P9-AZX-351

Cleopatra
CONFESSES

Also by Carolyn Meyer

Where the Broken Heart Still Beats:
The Story of Cynthia Ann Parker

White Lilacs

Rio Grande Stories

Drummers of Jericho

Gideon's People

Jubilee Journey

Mary, Bloody Mary

Isabel, Jewel of Castilla

Anastasia, The Last Grand Duchess

Beware, Princess Elizabeth

Kristina, The Girl King of Sweden

Doomed Queen Anne

Patience, Princess Catherine

Marie, Dancing

Loving Will Shakespeare

Duchessina: A Novel of Catherine de' Medici

In Mozart's Shadow: His Sister's Story

The True Adventures of Charley Darwin

The Bad Queen: Rules and Instructions
for Marie-Antoinette

CAROLYN
MEYER

A PAULA WISEMAN BOOK
SIMON & SCHUSTER BFYR
NEW YORK LONDON TORONTO SYDNEY

SIMON & SCHUSTER BFYR
An imprint of Simon & Schuster Children's Publishing Division
1230 Avenue of the Americas, New York, New York 10020

Book design by Krista Vossen
Map illustration by Drew Willis
The text for this book is set in Minion.
Manufactured in the United States of America
2 4 6 8 10 9 7 5 3 1
Library of Congress Cataloging-in-Publication Data
Meyer, Carolyn, 1935-
Cleopatra confesses / Carolyn Meyer. — 1st ed.
p. cm.
"A Paula Wiseman book."
Summary: Princess Cleopatra, the third (and favorite) daughter of King Ptolemy XII, comes of age in ancient Egypt, accumulating power and discovering love.
Includes bibliographical references (p. 282).
ISBN 978-1-4169-8727-7
1. Cleopatra, Queen of Egypt, d. 30 B.C.—Childhood and youth—Juvenile fiction. [1. Cleopatra, Queen of Egypt, d. 30 B.C.—Childhood and youth—Fiction. 2. Princesses—Fiction. 3. Kings, queens, rulers, etc.—Fiction. 4. Egypt—History—332-30 B.C.—Fiction.]
I. Title.
PZ7.M5685Cl 2011
[Fic]—dc22
2010025989
ISBN 978-1-4424-2245-2 (eBook)

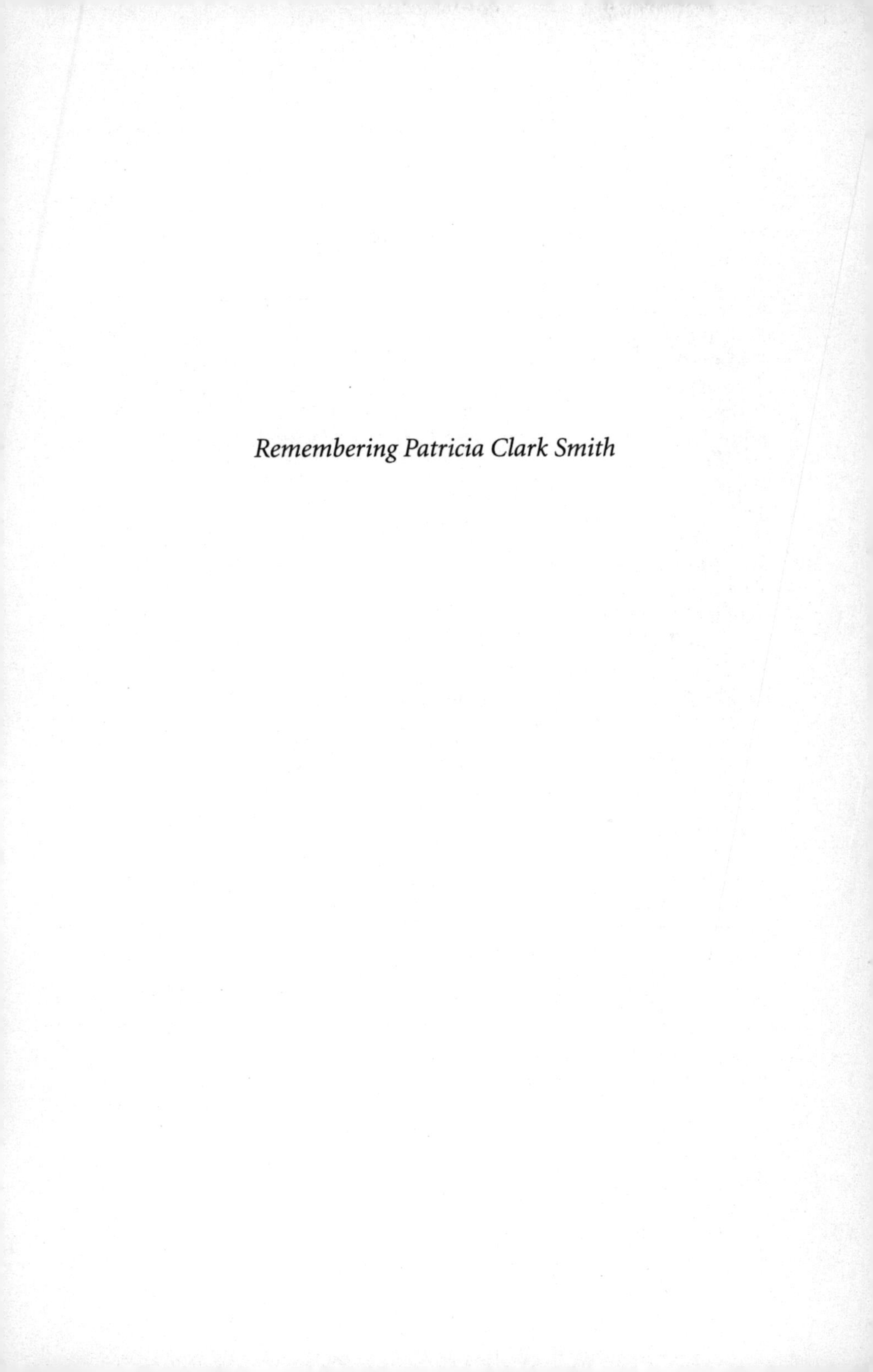

Remembering Patricia Clark Smith

Character List

Historical
Cleopatra VII
Ptolemy XII/Auletes, Cleopatra's father
Arsinoë, Cleopatra's younger sister
Tryphaena, Cleopatra's older sister
Berenike, Cleopatra's older sister
Ptolemy XIII, Cleopatra's younger brother
Ptolemy XIV, Cleopatra's younger brother
Crassus, wealthy Roman politician, member of triumvirate
Pompey, important Roman general, member of triumvirate
Julius Caesar, ambitious Roman general, most powerful member of triumvirate
Seleucus, Syrian guest of Ptolemy XII
Archelaus, son of king of Asia Minor
Dion of Alexandria, Egyptian philosopher and ambassador to Rome
Marcus Antonius/Mark Antony
Theodotus, tutor to Cleopatra's brothers
Achillas, Roman general, regent to Ptolemy XIII
Pothinus, regent to Ptolemy XIII
Yuya, Cleopatra's grand vizier
Ganymede, Arsinöe's tutor-guardian

Fictional *(characters added to help tell Cleopatra's story)*
Antiochus, grand vizier
Nebtawi, bodyguard
Ako, pet monkey
Panya, nurse
Irisi, servant
Monifa, servant
Demetrius, tutor
Captain Mshai, boat captain, father and son
Bubu, pet baboon
Akantha, niece of Antiochus
Charmion, dancer
Lady Amandaris, Charmion's mother
Titus, nephew of Antiochus
Nebibi, royal stablemaster
Bucephala, horse
Sepa, bodyguard
Hasani, bodyguard
Yafeu, messenger
Apollodorus, linen merchant

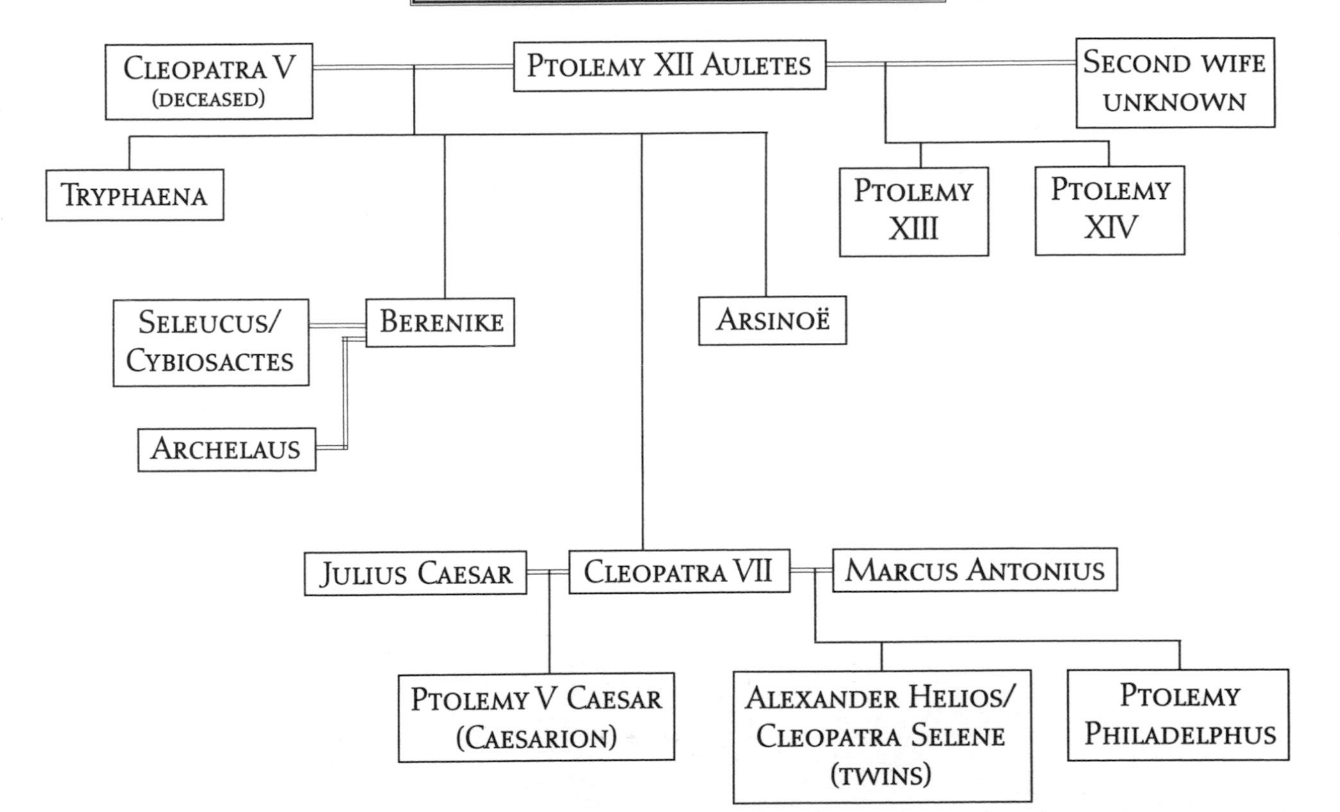
PTOLEMY FAMILY TREE
Cleopatra V
(deceased)
Ptolemy XII Auletes
Second wife unknown
Tryphaena
Ptolemy XIII
Ptolemy XIV
Seleucus/ Cybiosactes
Berenike
Arsinoë
Archelaus
Julius Caesar
Cleopatra VII
Marcus Antonius
Ptolemy V Caesar (Caesarion)
Alexander Helios/ Cleopatra Selene (twins)
Ptolemy Philadelphus

Ancient Egypt
and Lands of the Mediterranean

Prologue

My enemy stands at the gates of my city, Alexandria, in Egypt. The messenger tells me I have not much time before Octavian will arrive at the door of my magnificent tomb, where I have taken refuge. I have expected him. I know what he wants: to take me to Rome as a prisoner and parade me in chains, to dishonor me.

I am in my thirty-ninth year, and I have prepared well for the moment when I will leave my earthly life behind. My crowns as queen of Upper and Lower Egypt, my splendid robes and fabled jewels, quantities of fine food and wine and rare perfumes and oils to last an eternity—everything I could need or want.

Many of those I loved and who shared my life have gone before me, and soon I, too, will die. For the present, I sit alone. Before the end of day, Octavian will come, demanding to see me. I wait for him. I am Queen of Egypt, the most powerful woman ever to rule Egypt, yet I cannot save myself.

But what memories I have and what stories I can tell! Listen, then, to my stories of love and hate, passion and bitterness, envy, greed, ambition—I have experienced them all—and I will explain to you a world so different from yours, and yet in some ways so much the same.

I begin in my childhood, when I am ten years old; by our reckoning, Year 23 in the reign of my father, King Ptolemy XII. On your calendar it is 59 B.C., *fifty-nine years before the birth of Christ.*

Part I

The King of Egypt

Alexandria, beginning in my tenth year

Chapter 1

King Ptolemy XII

It is the season of Inundation, the time of year when the Nile overflows its banks, flooding the fields and renewing them for planting. The royal palace is quiet. I, the king's third daughter, called Cleopatra, am ten years old. I sit alone in my quarters, reading the scroll laid out on my table. I am nearly halfway through a history by my favorite Greek writer, Herodotus, when I hear a commotion in the forecourt. I abandon the scroll and step outside to investigate.

Glistening with sweat, a runner bows low before me and delivers his message. A lookout has sighted the royal fleet outside the entrance to the Great Harbor. My father, Ptolemy XII, the king of Egypt, is returning to Alexandria. This is the news I have longed for. He has been away for many months. Word reached Egypt that the king had left Rome, but much can happen to a ship crossing the vast sea called the Mediterranean.

A dozen runners have sprinted across the causeway from the lighthouse, the swiftest dispatched to the royal palace to relay the news to the king's household, beginning with his grand vizier, Antiochus. The grand vizier is no doubt sleeping, having finished duck hunting in the cooler hours of the morning. He will not like having his rest disturbed.

Next, the king's children are informed, starting with my older sisters, Tryphaena and Berenike, followed by me and then by Arsinoë, who is eight—two years younger than I—and, finally, the nurses who care for our little brothers. I hurry to look for Arsinoë. She is plump and affectionate but not the least bit clever. She will be glad to see Father, though he has never paid much attention to her. He had not wanted a fourth daughter.

I find Arsinoë playing with her pet monkey, Ako, under the watchful eye of her devoted bodyguard, Nebtawi. My sister has dressed Ako in a little kilt and is dancing it around like a furry doll. The monkey screeches, breaks free, and leaps onto me, flinging its hairy arms around my neck. Annoyed, I pry it off, and it scampers away, still wearing the ridiculous kilt. In two long strides Nebtawi captures the runaway and tenderly returns it to Arsinoë. My sister beams at her bodyguard. He is a short, muscular eunuch, and they are almost like father and daughter.

"Father is coming today," Arsinoë announces. "I've already heard. Panya says I may wear a new dress and jewels but that I may not use cosmetics." Her lower lip is already forming a pout. Panya has been my sister's nurse since our mother died giving birth to Arsinoë, and she is very protective.

"You still have your sidelock," I remind her, looking at the long lock of hair hanging from her head, the mark of childhood. "No cosmetics until it is cut off."

"When will that be?" she asks, although surely she already knows.

"When you start to grow breasts."

I lost my sidelock only a month earlier, though I was not quite ready. More than a little, but I wish to be taken seriously and not treated like a child.

"Your hair is growing faster than your breasts," my sister Tryphaena had said with a sneer when I first appeared without my sidelock. My eyes had welled with tears, though I refused to let her see them.

I leave Arsinoë with Nebtawi and her monkey and consider visiting my older sisters to take the measure of their mood, but I decide against it. I am not at all fond of them, nor are they of me. Tryphaena is sixteen, Berenike fourteen, and they have been jealous of me for as long as I can remember. It is because of Father. Sometimes they hint darkly that I am not even his true daughter. "You are not like us, Cleopatra," Berenike has said. They are right to believe that I am his favorite. But this is not my fault. I have done nothing to win his favor. Nevertheless, I avoid both of them.

They are probably taking their ease in the garden outside their quarters, as they do most days. Those two will not be happy to learn of Father's return. The longer the king stays away, the more likely they are to find a way to put themselves in his place. Nothing would have pleased them more than to learn that he was lost at sea. But now he has come back, and they will be forced to put on a good face and pretend to welcome him. It will be an interesting performance to watch.

Our little brothers, one barely two years old and the other born after my father left for Rome and not yet weaned, are not old enough to care. It is the custom among royal families of Egypt to use names over and over, even within one generation, so our little brothers, Ptolemy XIII and Ptolemy XIV, are named for Father. My mother, Father's first wife, was Cleopatra V, and Tryphaena is known formally as Cleopatra VI. I am Cleopatra VII. The name means "Famous in her Father." I believe it suits *me* best.

It has also been the custom of the pharaohs since the earliest days of Egypt for royal brothers to marry their sisters. My mother was Father's half sister. I remember hardly anything about my mother, except her lovely voice and her scent. Sometimes I catch a hint of perfume that brings back a memory of her as hard to grasp as a winter mist, and her absence often makes me feel alone, though there are people everywhere around me. Father later remarried, hoping for sons, but only weeks after the birth of Ptolemy XIV, the grand vizier delivered a letter to the queen from the king, divorcing her. The grand vizier made sure the former queen moved out of the palace at once, leaving the two youngest Ptolemies in the care of their nurses. I felt a little sad for her, but not much. My stepmother had a cruel mouth and no fondness for me or for any of my father's daughters. And so no queen now waits to embrace King Ptolemy, but Father will not be lonely. At least a dozen young women of the court are eager to welcome him.

I return to my quarters. My servants, Irisi and Monifa, are not there. Monifa, who has been caring for me since my birth, is like a mother to me. Irisi is younger, closer to my age, but not close enough to be a true friend. Taking advantage of their absence, I choose a coarse linen tunic from Irisi's chest and wrap one of her plain kerchiefs over my hair, fastening it with two of my own gold hairpins. With Monifa's market basket slung over my arm as if I were going to buy bread, I slip out of my rooms. I want to be at the harbor when the royal ships arrive.

The king will not make his formal entry into Alexandria in the heat of the day. He will have ordered his ships to lie some distance offshore until the sun god, Ra, hangs low in the western sky and word of the king's return has reached every quarter of the city and the excitement has had a chance to build. There is plenty of time.

But the grand vizier happens to see me and steps into my path. "Where are you going, Princess Cleopatra?" he asks.

"To watch for Father's ship."

Antiochus is tall and thin with a gleaming shaved head and ears that stick out like the handles on a wine jar. In the king's absence the grand vizier has done hardly anything but amuse himself with hunting and gambling. I know he disapproves of my frequent escapes away from the royal quarter and into the world of ordinary Egyptians, but he has never tried to stop me. I am sure he will cause me no trouble, for I am aware of a few facts about him that he would prefer to keep secret. For instance, I know that he regularly pilfers the royal storehouse to pay off his gambling debts. We have an unspoken bargain between us. Antiochus frowns and moves aside.

The palace guards ignore me as I walk boldly past them and make my way through the back streets, avoiding the broad avenues. I have been making these unapproved visits to the marketplace since Father left for Rome. No one takes any notice of a ten-year-old girl dressed in servant's clothes. If they knew my true identity, it would be otherwise. Princesses are not expected to roam the city alone, without a retinue of servants and bodyguards.

I can see that the royal fleet is still just a handful of dots on the horizon, well beyond the great Pharos lighthouse, which guides ships past the treacherous coast and into the harbor, but the whole city is already wide awake. Before the sun has climbed even halfway to the midpoint of the heavens, preparations are well under way for the king's arrival. Assistants to the grand vizier sit beneath an awning in the marketplace, giving orders. Workers carry rolls of thick carpet for the king to walk on. Others are draping a special platform with silks from the Orient, attaching torches to tall poles, and hoisting bright pennants that snap in the stiff breeze blowing steadily off the sea. Welcoming speeches will be delivered from that platform by Antiochus and the highest-ranking noblemen. The crowd will be eager to hear news of King Ptolemy's journey to Rome.

Before my father sailed for that faraway city more than a year ago, he had explained to me what he hoped to accomplish there.

"I am going for the sake of Egypt," he said. "Rome would like nothing better than to take over our country. They claim to have legal rights to it, and the Romans are formidable—they could do it easily. That would mean the end of Egypt as an independent country and the end of my kingship. There would be no more pharaohs ruling here, no more Ptolemies, only three Romans who hold all the authority—two generals and a public official. I spit on them! And yet I must fawn over them and pretend friendship. Those three men will determine what happens to Egypt, and I must convince them to support me as the rightful ruler of the land."

Father spoke to me that night as he always did, using the familiar form, as a father speaks to his children. He took it for granted I would understand, though I was just nine years old when he left and not clear on the details. Now I wonder if he has persuaded those three men—the triumvirate—to recognize that he is Egypt's true pharaoh.

It must have been obvious to everybody, not just my sisters, that I am my father's favorite. "You are his precious jewel," they say sourly, with curled lips. I do not disagree with them. They believe this not because he gives me costly gifts—he gives them such gifts too. They demand them! They believe it because I am the daughter he always chose to be by his side, who rode with him into the desert and sailed with him on Lake Mareotis, who accompanied him whenever he entertained visitors and cheered him when he was alone.

Monifa, who knows me as well as my father does, claims that he favors me because, of all his children, I am most like him. "You have his keen intelligence," she once told me, "and his ability to persuade, as well as his strength of purpose."

Her words fill me with pride, but I cannot resist pressing her to tell me more about my parents. "And my mother?" I ask. "Do I resemble her?"

"You do not look like her," Monifa says firmly. "Your sisters more closely resemble her in their features." Monifa no doubt sees the disappointment written on my face. "I see only your father in your eyes and the shape of your nose. But I do hear your mother in your voice. Her speech fell like music on his ears. It enchanted him and melted his heart. Yours does the same."

Her answers delight me. I am pleased, of course, by my special status, but the situation could mean trouble. I know that being the favorite could put me in danger.

Here is why: Tryphaena and Berenike are determined to

be next in line to rule Egypt. They talk about it constantly, saying such things as "When we are on the throne" or "When Father is no longer king." They never come right out and say "When Auletes is dead," but I know my sisters, and I am uneasy about their intentions. They may see me as an obstacle blocking their path.

"Auletes" is an epithet meaning "Flute Player," a name bestowed on Father by his subjects, who did not intend it kindly. He prefers to be known as the New Dionysus, the Greek god of wine, the inspirer of ecstasy. Both names fit him well. He likes to play the *aulos*, a long, finely carved ivory flute, especially when he has drunk too much wine. Sometimes he dances in honor of Dionysus while he plays. He has been doing that for as long as I can remember. I love the music and dancing, but my older sisters are not amused. They call him Auletes behind his back, never to his face.

"He's a fool," says Berenike.

"A drunken idiot," Tryphaena adds.

I disagree, but I say nothing. Father is certainly neither a fool nor an idiot, but he is a man of many contradictions. I would rather think of his intelligence and his good humor and forgive his faults. His greatest weakness is his fondness for grand feasts, which sometimes causes him to neglect his duties as king.

It is my sisters who are fools. They are jealous not only of me but also of each other. Tryphaena assumes she will be the next queen and boasts about the luxuries she will enjoy—as though she is not already completely spoiled! Her name means "Ostentatious Pleasure Lover"—fitting, I think. Although she is the eldest, she is not the ablest or the most intelligent of my sisters. That would be Berenike, who is also sure that *she* is the one who will be queen. I will not be surprised if those two someday tear each other's eyes out in a jealous rage. It would be wise to gamble on Berenike. She has a ruthless streak that makes her more dangerous than Tryphaena.

I believe that someday I could become a great ruler of Egypt, better than my sisters can dream of being, but I must be careful not to let them know how I feel. I do not want them to see me as a rival for the throne and a threat to their plans. With Father away on a long journey, it would have been an easy matter for them to arrange my disappearance.

Now Father has returned. But is he safe, or are my sisters actually plotting against him? If they are, then my life, too, may be in peril.

Chapter 2

Homecoming

The dots on the horizon grow larger. Now I can make out the striped sails. It is the hottest part of the day, but the excitement is growing. People from every quarter of the great city are gathering near the harbor—mostly Egyptians, but also Cypriots, Syrians, Jews, and of course my people, the Greeks. We are the descendants of Philip of Macedonia, the northern part of Greece. It has been nearly three hundred years since Philip's son, Alexander the Great, liberated Egypt from the Persian occupiers and laid out the city as his new capital. Alexander's half brother and favorite general, Ptolemy, became the first of the new line of pharaohs to rule Egypt; my father is the twelfth to bear the name. Like their ancestors going back thousands of years, the people now flocking to welcome him believe their pharaoh is a demigod, half divine and half human. It is impossible for me to imagine they might someday accept my two silly, vain, empty-headed sisters as their rulers. Surely the people of Egypt deserve better.

I leave the shade of a colonnaded porch and plunge into the sprawling marketplace. Sellers of spices and medicines, dealers in religious charms, makers of sturdy sandals and useless trinkets, bakers and brewers—all are jammed together here under shade cloths, all shouting out their wares. I wander among them, listening. Greek is the language of my family, from my Macedonian ancestors to the present day, as it is of most of the wealthy nobility, but I also understand Egyptian, the language of the servants in the palace and the workers and vendors in the streets. I enjoy being among the common people, unrecognized, not only to escape the dull routine of my life in the palace, but to savor the exciting sights and sounds of the city. My sisters would think I am stupid—they love the attention they attract. And my father, if he knew, surely would not approve.

An old woman, blind in one eye, stirs a large pot of stew over a brazier and sings out, "Good food! Good food today!" My mouth waters at the delicious smell of her cooking, but there is a problem: I have no coins with which to buy anything. It is assumed that a royal princess has no need for money. Then I remember the two simple gold pins I used to fasten my kerchief. Maybe I can trade one of them for a bowl of stew.

I pull a pin from my kerchief and offer it to the old woman. "A bowl of stew, if you please," I say in her language. I have learned the Egyptian language very well.

She glances at me sharply and inspects the hairpin, holding it close to her good eye. Then she thrusts the pin back into my hand. "You stole this," she announces in a cracked old voice.

"No, no," I assure her. "I did not steal it. It is mine. I have nothing else to give you." I hold out the pin again. "Please take it. Your stew smells so good, and I am very hungry." I rub my stomach to make my point.

"Hunh," she snorts, glaring at me suspiciously. But she snatches the hairpin and thrusts it into the folds of her frayed tunic. Picking up one of the clay bowls stacked on the ground beside her, she fills it with a thick mixture of lentils and onions and herbs, and shoves it at me with a chunk of bread. I carry my bowl to a low wall and sit down to eat, using the bread to sop up the juices.

The old woman does a brisk business. Scribes in long skirts come from their offices, and laborers wearing only loincloths lay aside their tools. Many customers are drivers of the donkey carts that carry loads of firewood over the causeway to the lighthouse. The donkeys must drag their heavy loads up a long, winding ramp to a furnace at the top of the tower, where an enormous polished bronze mirror reflects the fire and beams the bright light out to sea. The Pharos lighthouse, the most famous in the world, is taller than anything I have ever seen.

"The light can be seen from a great distance. It will lead me home," Father said. And it has.

While I eat, I listen to the clamor of voices around me. Laborers grumble about their cruel overseers; overseers find fault with the lazy laborers. All protest the new taxes imposed by the grand vizier, Antiochus. "We have nothing left with which to feed our families when Antiochus is done with us!" cries a man wearing a ragged loincloth, and others nod their agreement, adding their own bitter complaints.

It is true. I can see with my own eyes that the common people of Alexandria do not live well. They blame Antiochus, but I wonder if it was Father who ordered the taxes.

The old woman keeps her good eye on me while she serves the crowd. When I finish, I wipe my greasy hands on Irisi's tunic—at the palace a servant would have been waiting with a pitcher of warm water to wash my hands—and return the empty bowl to the pile. The old woman refills it and hands it to her next customer.

As I start to walk away, the woman calls out. Reaching inside her tunic, she retrieves the gold hairpin. "Here, take this. It is no use to me. Someone will say I stole it." She waves me off impatiently when I try to protest. "You liked my stew well enough, little princess?" she asks slyly.

"Never has food tasted better," I assure her. *Has she recognized me?* I wonder.

"Good," she says. "Your words are all I need." She squints at me, head cocked to one side. "I have heard that one of the royal princesses speaks the language of our people," she adds. "I did not believe it, but now I do."

She is right—I have learned not only the Egyptian language but several others. Once I hear a language spoken, it becomes a part of me without much effort. I nod and smile. "It is our secret."

"Yes, our secret," she says with a nearly toothless smile. "You come to me whenever you are hungry, little princess, and I will make sure your stomach is filled." She turns away, calling out, "Good food! Praise to the great god Osiris, King Ptolemy is coming home! Have some good food today!"

The crowd is growing; soon the old woman's pot will be empty. Laborers stop to refresh themselves with beer from a neighboring stall. Street dancers entertain the crowds. Boats filled with flowers and gifts of fruit dart around the harbor, and some of the larger ones venture out through the waves that dash against the shore, sending up foaming sprays of water. The hours pass as we await the king's arrival. The sun balances delicately on the horizon before it begins its quick descent. It is time for me to go back to the palace. King Ptolemy will make his formal entrance into the city after darkness falls.

Irisi and Monifa are waiting for me, fidgeting nervously. "It worries us when you go out alone," Monifa frets. "We are always afraid some harm will come to you."

Irisi undresses me, stripping off the borrowed tunic. "Look at my tunic!" she cries. "What were you doing, Cleopatra?"

"Eating stew. It was delicious."

I stand obediently in the bathing room while the two women pour jars of warm water over me and scrub me clean with sponges. "What dirty feet!" Monifa grumbles.

Dried with soft cloths and rubbed with scented oil, I let my servants dress me in a narrow sheath of fine white royal linen held up with shoulder straps. They tie a bright-colored sash around my waist, the fringes falling nearly to my ankles. They strap handsomely worked leather sandals on my feet and fasten a pair of gold bracelets on my upper arms and a collar made of glazed beads and lapis lazuli around my neck. The hairdresser comes to fix my hair, and the face painter touches my lips and cheeks with red ochre. Monifa drapes an intricately pleated linen cloth over my shoulders.

The women look me over carefully. "King Ptolemy will find his third daughter quite pleasing, I am sure," says Irisi. She smiles and bows, and I touch her shoulder affectionately.

I am ready to greet my beloved father.

Chapter 3

FATHER

It is evening, well past sunset on the day of Father's return. Torches blaze along the broad avenues. We ride from the palace in gilded sedan chairs borne by carriers wearing decorated leather aprons. My older sisters are dressed in linen sheaths similar to mine. They must have emptied their jewel chests to adorn themselves with as many precious gems as possible. The hairdresser and face painter have done lavish work on them, outlining their eyes with black kohl and brushing a green powder on their eyelids. My sisters preen and smile. They probably think they are very beautiful, but to me they seem false, like painted statues.

We take our places on the platform among heaps of flowers and gifts brought by noble families. Glowing lanterns swing from the masts of the royal ships now anchored in the Great Harbor. The cheering grows to a roar. There he is! The king, my father! My throat swells with pride and my skin prickles with excitement.

Wearing the double crown of Egypt and a lion's tail slung around his waist, King Ptolemy XII stands proudly with his hands on his hips and his feet planted wide as he is rowed to shore in a gilded boat with flashing silver oars. He climbs ashore on a carved wooden ramp and mounts the platform. Each of his daughters, beginning with Tryphaena, the eldest, steps forward and bows low before him, bent almost double at the waist, and touches his feet. He does not speak, and his expression reveals nothing of how he feels. Berenike is next.

It is my turn. *Something is troubling him*, I think, glancing at my father as I step forward. *He has let his hair grow, and it is streaked with gray.* I offer my formal greeting, "Welcome, my father, my king, my lord," though I am longing to say so much more: *I have missed you terribly. I am so glad you are here.* He acknowledges me with a faint smile and a slight nod. I had hoped for more of a response from him after our long separation, but I understand that this is a ceremonial occasion. Perhaps later he will tell me how much he missed me, how happy he is to see me again.

Stepping back, I wonder what Tryphaena and Berenike are thinking. Do they also sense that something is wrong? There is no way to guess from the false smiles pasted on their painted faces.

Arsinoë bounces on her toes, grinning stupidly, until I grab her and pull her to my side. Two high-ranking women who obviously know nothing about babies—they probably never cared for their own—present my little brothers to their father. The women kneel so that the infants can reach out their chubby hands and touch the pharaoh's foot. The little Ptolemies begin screaming, my father looks perplexed, and the noblewomen hurry to hand off their squalling charges to the children's nurses.

The formal greetings end, poems are recited and hymns sung in praise of the pharaoh. So far the king has not spoken a word. It is his right, as pharaoh and demigod, to remain silent and let his presence speak for him. The procession starts down the Canopic Way. The broadest avenue in the world, as everyone says, it is paved with slabs of granite and lined with twin rows of marble columns, each column so thick that three men can barely join hands around a single one of them.

King Ptolemy rides at the head in a golden chariot drawn by a pair of high-stepping white horses. We follow in our gilded chairs, past the beautiful tomb of our ancestor, Alexander the Great. Behind us comes a crowd of noblemen and their wives. When we reach the Gate of the Moon at the western end, the procession doubles back on itself. The result is chaos, a churning sea of people. After what seems a very long time, we reach the palace to begin the night's feasting.

Berenike glares at me through narrowed eyes. "Well, I suppose you're happy, Cleopatra," she says in a voice like sour wine, "now that your dear father has come back."

I stare at my sister. "Of course I'm happy," I reply. "Aren't you?"

"I thought we did quite well without him," she snaps.

"And I agree," adds Tryphaena. "Quite well indeed. But you're too young to understand."

I open my mouth, ready to argue. Then I change my mind. "Let us enjoy the banquet, dear sisters. For Father's sake."

Idle for a year, except for the occasional imperious demands of my sisters, the palace cooks have awakened as though from a long sleep and prepared a magnificent meal to celebrate the king's homecoming: whole oryxes roasted on spits, bowls heaped with pomegranates, grapes, and plums, bread flavored with cardamom and other spices, cakes drenched in honey, and enormous jars of wine carried in from the royal storehouse. (That is another thing: Grand Vizier Antiochus has been helping himself to the king's wine.)

Reclining on cushions, Father's guests are served course after course, while lithe girls only a little older than I am perform exotic dances, bending and twisting, leaping and swaying to the music of lute, lyre, harp, and jingling sistrum. The dancers' long braids, weighted at the ends, swing rhythmically with their graceful movements.

They have scarcely finished their performance when my father rises to his feet. I expect him to make a speech of some kind. Instead, he produces his flute and begins to play, eyes closed, dancing to his own music as though in a dream. My older sisters sigh and grimace. Most of his guests ignore the man they call Auletes and signal for more food and drink.

I yearn for sleep. Then, unexpectedly, I find my father standing before me. He reaches out to me with his free hand. "Cleopatra," he says. That is all—just my name.

"Father! It has been so long—" But he has already turned away and begun again to play his flute. I want to tell him how happy I am that he has come home and, if I can, to whisper a warning that he may be in danger. *Later,* I think. He is home safely, and for now that has to be enough. I put my hand over my mouth to suppress a yawn. I would like to find a corner to sleep in, but that would be impolite. The celebration will probably go on until daybreak.

Chapter 4

WAITING

Father has been back for three days and spends his time closeted with the grand vizier. I am eager to know what took place in Rome during his long year's absence. I wonder. *What kind of agreement did King Ptolemy reach with those three men he calls the triumvirate?* But I have not seen him alone. He has not yet sent for me.

While I wait for a chance to speak with my father, I follow my familiar routine, caught up in my studies—mathematics, astronomy, and history. This pleases my tutor, Demetrius, a solemn man with bowlegs, a bald head, a big belly, and an appetite for food as great as his hunger for knowledge. Our city has long been famous for the great Library of Alexandria, which holds several hundred thousand papyrus scrolls, as well as for its place of learning—the Museion—and its scholars in many different fields. Demetrius is known to be one of the most learned.

History is his favorite subject, and he never tires of telling me stories of Alexander's military triumphs. Before he died at the age of thirty-two, Alexander conquered vast territories with his half brother Ptolemy often at his side. His exploits excite me, and I cannot hear enough of them. But now, more than anything, I want to hear what my father accomplished in Rome.

Demetrius has traveled to many parts of the world and speaks several languages. When I told him that I, too, wished to learn other languages, he found me the proper teachers. I began to work on Arabian, Aramaic, and Syrian. After Father left for Rome, I became interested in Latin and soon mastered the writing of it, though I do not yet speak it fluently.

Of my father's four daughters, I am the studious one. I learn easily and remember whatever I have been taught, soaking up information like a thirsty sponge. My tutor and I are well matched.

"You have a gift for learning," Demetrius says, and I glow in the light of his praise.

My sisters mock me for it. "How can you bear to study so much?" Tryphaena once asked, though she did not actually want to hear my explanation.

"No man will ever want to have anything to do with you!" Berenike informed me.

"And why not?" I asked curiously.

"No man wants to be around a woman he feels is more intelligent than he is," she replied in a superior tone, inspecting her polished nails.

"Then you should have no trouble at all in finding men of every sort," I retorted, exchanging insult for insult and succeeding in infuriating her.

And that is how things now stand between us. My sisters are jealous and cannot help showing it. They resent me for being Father's favorite—his "precious jewel"—but they do not fear me. Not yet. I believe they fear each other, for each wants to be queen. For that reason, I will never admit to them that I, too, want to be queen. If they suspected, I would become another rival to be eliminated. But I keep this knowledge to myself.

Time seemed to crawl by while Father was gone. According to our calendar, there are three seasons—Inundation, when the Nile floods each year; Emergence, when the waters recede and crops are planted; and Harvest. Each season lasts four months, with each month made up of thirty days. There are also the five days of the Opening of the Year. Father was away for a full year plus one month. Every day that he was gone, I thought of him and missed him sorely.

Shortly after my father sailed for Rome, I peppered Demetrius with questions about the triumvirate and what claim the Romans have on Egypt. Demetrius would not give me a direct answer but instead waved away my queries like a swarm of annoying insects.

"We must all wait and see what happens, Cleopatra," he said, tucking his little chin into several layers of fat.

Now that Father has come back, I will pose my questions directly to him. I believe Father will answer me truthfully. I have not yet had a chance to talk to him. It has been three days, and I am impatient. But that is the way of kings.

Each night, Father entertains his friends at a banquet with feasting and music. I attend the banquets, but still I do not get to see him alone. I know it is not my place to speak to him first. When another day passes without a summons from my father, I decide to pay a visit to my sisters. Usually I try to avoid such unpleasant visits. But I can often learn from them.

I find Tryphaena and Berenike lounging in the garden under the spreading branches of an old sycamore. Water trickles through a series of bronze bowls, placed one beneath the other, and into a pond that is home to a number of fish. A trio of cats sit by the pond, ignoring the flickers of orange and yellow among the water lilies. A servant stirs the sultry air with a fan of ostrich feathers. A young girl kneels nearby with a platter of dates. My sisters are sipping from silver goblets.

"It seems we have a visitor," Berenike drawls. "Do join us, sister."

I sit down on a marble bench, and Tryphaena signals the servants to bring me a goblet. "So?" she asks, arching her eyebrows, which have been plucked into a fine line and blackened.

"Father looks well, don't you agree?" I ask, trying to sound offhand.

Berenike stuffs a date into her mouth and licks her fingers. "Why shouldn't he?"

"I thought perhaps the voyage might have tired him," I suggest.

"It's not as though he had to *row*, Cleopatra," she sneers.

A servant fills my goblet from a pitcher of sweet pomegranate juice. From the corner of my eye I catch a flash of color, the quick swipe of a paw, a splash of water. The cat cleans her whiskers, appearing unconcerned. *That is how my sisters would like to see it happen with Father*, I think. *A sudden disappearance.*

"Have you any idea what Father has done?" Berenike asks sharply.

I dislike admitting that I do not. "He hasn't spoken to me as yet," I confess. The edge in her voice worries me.

"He hasn't spoken to us, either, so we have no idea what agreement he made with the Romans. But he can't keep it a secret for long." Berenike glances at Tryphaena. "We have spies, you know." She leans toward me, eyes glittering. "They're everywhere. No one can keep secrets from us—not even *you*, Cleopatra."

I consider myself warned. I drain my goblet, and having learned nothing of interest from my sneering sisters, as soon as I can get away from them, I do.

I sense treachery in these two. I cannot bear to be near them.

Chapter 5

CONVERSATION

Nine days after his return, following a banquet that ended earlier than most, Father enters my quarters and announces that he will speak to me—*now*. He has never done this. I worry: Have I somehow displeased him?

Irisi, wide eyed at this unexpected visit, helps me dress hurriedly, and I go out to greet him, bowing low and touching his feet.

"Ah, Cleopatra!" He sighs. "You're growing up! How much you've changed in a year! How old are you now?"

"Ten years," I tell him. "I will be eleven in the third month of Emergence, on the Festival of Isis," I remind him.

He studies me carefully, shaking his head. "Time passes so quickly."

Father climbs the stairs to the roof of the palace, and I understand that I am expected to follow. When a servant appears with a bowl of fruit, he orders her to leave it and waves her away.

Father's mood seems serious, even sad. Perhaps now he will tell me what I want to know. He does not explain why he has come here so late at night. But it is not up to me to ask questions. I remind myself again that I must wait. I must learn patience. We sit quietly, saying nothing, listening to the cry of a night bird. I nibble on a slice of melon, though I am not at all hungry.

"Cleopatra, my daughter," he begins at last. "I know you're wondering what transpired in Rome. Tonight I shall tell you everything. I'll answer all your questions. And then I don't wish to speak of it again."

"As you desire, Father." Out of respect, I am careful to speak to him in formal language, not the familiar speech he uses with me.

He describes the long and difficult sea journey, in which he followed the coast toward the setting sun, beloved Egypt always on his left hand, then turned northward, and later crossed open water to reach the island of Sicily. "Fierce storms tossed the fleet about like bits of wood, and one ship was lost. I'm not a man of the sea. I prefer to look at it from the shore," he says with a wry smile. "But that wasn't the end of it. We encountered more storms on the way to Ostia, the harbor city of Rome. Another ship went down before we reached our destination."

He gazes out at the dark sea, his thoughts far away, before he continues.

"First, you should know about the triumvirate, the three most powerful men in Rome, to whom special attention must be paid," Father says. I lean toward him, listening intently. "Crassus is a rich man who has been waiting to annex Egypt for years. He is avid for our abundant grain to feed the growing population of his country. The second man is an important general known as Pompey the Great. He befriended me when I needed his support, and in fact I grew fond of him."

Father falls silent. The only sound is of the sea, wave after wave pounding against the breakwater. All my life I have been lulled to sleep by that sound. Now it seems not soothing but ominous. My father says nothing for so long, I believe he must have forgotten me.

"And the third, Father?" I prompt gently. "Who is the third Roman in this triumvirate?"

"Julius Caesar," Father replies, "by far the most ambitious of the three. The others fear Caesar's power, but they respect him too." He rises and begins to pace restlessly. "I gave them gifts," he says. "Very large gifts."

"As their guest you were expected to give them gifts, were you not?"

"I promised them six thousand talents. That was the basis of our agreement."

"Six thousand talents!" I gape at him, openmouthed. "That is an enormous sum, Father!"

"Enormous indeed. More than half of Egypt's revenue for an entire year—an entire *good* year. But Antiochus tells me that it has not been a good year for Egypt. Last year's flood was far less than expected, and as a result the crops failed to flourish and the harvest was poor. This season's flood was no better. Farmers in the Nile Valley earn very little for their labors, and they complain that our high taxes are the ruin of them."

"I have heard such complaints in the marketplace." I should not have said that, but Father does not ask what I was doing there. He probably thinks I was visiting in the company of my tutor.

"You are likely to hear many more." Father sits down suddenly and stares at the floor. "Pompey insisted that I give them their gift immediately."

I may be young, but I understand very well how money is used to gain favor. Bribes are the accepted way of getting things done. But this is much more than a bribe. It is almost as though Father gave them a huge piece of the kingdom. *But what did he gain in return?* I nod and listen, saying nothing, waiting for an explanation.

"The only way I could meet Pompey's demands was to borrow the entire amount from a Roman moneylender. To repay six thousand talents, plus all the interest due, I must order everyone in Egypt to pay much higher taxes. The people will hate me for it—they are already overburdened. I have to convince them that I did what is best for our country."

I still do not understand. Why would my father give away so much of Egypt's treasure? I ask him quietly, "What did the Romans give you in return, Father?"

"Julius Caesar promised to leave Egypt alone, and the triumvirs will continue to recognize me as the pharaoh. I have Caesar's word, though I am not sure I can trust him."

My father puts his head down in his arms and begins to weep. I have never seen him so distraught. I want to believe that my father really has acted for the good of our country, but I wonder if the people of Egypt will be as understanding. Some are sure to believe he did it only to keep himself in power.

We have been talking for so long that the stars have begun to fade. I creep close and lay my hand lightly on Father's shoulder, but he shrugs it off. "Leave me, Cleopatra!" he groans, and obediently I tiptoe away.

Chapter 6

Festival of Isis

It is winter now, and the winds sweeping in from the sea are bitter. Father has been back in Alexandria for four months. Today, the Festival of Isis, I am eleven years old. At the banquet honoring the great goddess of fertility and motherhood and also of magic, Father calls upon me to be recognized by our guests. I stand by his side and smile and even manage to say a few words in praise of Isis, though I am not at ease speaking before a large crowd of people who would rather be talking among themselves or enjoying the dancers. When I have finished my brief speech, Father announces his plan to begin a journey by royal boat up the Nile, stopping at towns and cities to greet his subjects and to make offerings at the temples of the gods. He intends to go as far as the First Cataract, where the river is shallow, the bottom is rough, and huge boulders block a boat's passage. My sisters and I will accompany him, and most of the members of the court present at this banquet will join the party as well.

"We will all enjoy a journey to warmer places," he says. I understand that the real reason is to show himself to the people and remind them that he is their pharaoh.

Preparations begin at once for our large entourage—as many as a hundred noblemen and their wives and servants—to set out near the end of the fourth month of the season of Emergence as the crops along the river are nearly finished ripening. The journey will be a long one, likely lasting through the four months of Harvest, until summer begins, and perhaps even longer.

I am delighted. I have never before traveled with Father. I had begged him to take me with him to Rome, but he refused, saying, "A voyage of this kind is no place for you, Cleopatra. You are too young to be faced with the dangers of sea travel." I was only nine then. But now that I am eleven I wonder if he would consider me old enough to accompany him on such a voyage, if he decides to make another. I long to travel to distant places, but in fact I have seldom been outside Alexandria.

Arsinoë is excited too, so long as her monkey will be allowed to come with us. But our disagreeable older sisters pull long faces.

"Four months on a boat! It will be too boring," Berenike complains.

"Unbearably dull," Tryphaena agrees. "We have much more interesting things to do here in Alexandria. Don't we, Berenike?"

The two exchange glances, and I wonder what they are plotting. "No doubt you look forward to the journey, Cleopatra," Berenike says archly. "Father will surely want to have his precious jewel to display wherever he goes."

"I am not his precious jewel!" I retort, and immediately regret allowing her to see how easily she can annoy me.

I have not seen much of my older sisters since Father returned. The royal palace compound is large and sprawling, with many separate parts, and we each have our own small palaces, our own servants and tutors and bodyguards. My sisters certainly do not seek me out. Father expects us to attend his dinners when he entertains guests—that is nearly every night—and we manage to be polite when we meet there. But it will be much harder to keep my distance from my sisters on a boat, even one as large as the king's.

Neither have I seen much of my father during these preparations. He spends most of his days with Antiochus and his other advisors, and at night there are the banquets. We have had no more private conversations. In less than a month we are ready to embark on our journey up the Nile. Perhaps now he will have time for me.

Part II

The Nile

On the river, during my eleventh year

Chapter 7

THE ROYAL BOAT

Before we leave Alexandria to begin our journey, my father, my sisters, and I climb a hundred steps to reach the beautiful golden-roofed temple built to honor the god Serapis, protector of the city. Set on the highest point in Alexandria, the temple houses the statue of Serapis, brought here from Greece by the first Ptolemy. The enormous statue with curly hair and beard has a basket of grain on its head; at its feet sits the snarling three-headed dog, Cerberus, a frightening figure that sends Arsinoë to huddle close by my side. We leave our offerings—mine is the blue-glazed figure of a hedgehog—and descend the stairs. Our bearers are waiting to carry us in our chairs to the royal boat, which is anchored in Lake Mareotis, south of the ancient city walls.

When my sisters and I were still young children, Father gave us each a boat just large enough to carry a princess and a small entourage of servants and oarsmen. I have sailed on these calm lake waters many times on my own little boat. But this is the first time I or any of my sisters have been a passenger on the king's vessel.

The king's royal boat is an awesome sight, built of rare cypress and cedar brought here from Lebanon. It is some two hundred cubits long and thirty cubits wide—a cubit being the distance from the elbow to the tip of the middle finger—and gilded from end to end. It will take me days to explore it all.

The king's boat lacks nothing. A palace built on the smooth wooden deck has an open area sheltered from the sun by striped awnings. The dining hall, its walls hung with crimson silk and its floors tiled with polished stone, is large enough to seat about two hundred guests. Trees and flowering gardens line the paved walkways, and bright-colored fishes dart about a reflecting pool. There are shrines to the great goddess Isis and to Father's favorite deity, Dionysus. Each of us has our own large apartment with quarters for our servants. My trunks of clothes and jewels are already in place. Demetrius and the other tutors who accompany us share quarters. Father says we must continue our studies, though I am sure my sisters will avoid it if they possibly can.

Dozens of luxurious small boats decorated with pennants and flowers are fitted out to carry the noblemen and their wives. Cooks and servants and the musicians and dancers who will entertain us travel on smaller, crowded boats. Barges manned by oarsmen will tow the royal boat through the canals and pull it when the winds are not strong enough to drive it upstream against the current.

The oarsmen bend their backs to the rhythm of a muffled drumbeat. The boats cross the lake and enter a canal leading to the Canopus, the most western of the seven branches of the Nile that stretch like fingers northward toward the sea. Soon we are in the great swampy river delta, where men are cutting down tall, feathery papyrus reeds and loading them onto rafts. Wading birds stalk through the reeds on thin, naked legs. Geese and ducks rise into the air on a whirr of wings, and boys propel little papyrus boats through the shallow water with long poles and shoot at the water fowl with bows and arrows. Crocodiles with dark bronze backs glide by, only their green eyes glowing above the surface.

Arsinoë, watching with me, shudders. "I'm afraid of them," she says, pointing at the crocodiles, and I put my arm around her shoulders to comfort her. She seems so young and innocent, lacking our older sisters' hard outer shell and inner selfishness and pride.

Then Demetrius summons me to my studies. "You must not waste your time simply gazing at the scenery, Cleopatra," he says. "We shall concentrate on mathematics, the area where I find you to be weakest."

He is wrong about that; I am not weak in any area. But I enjoy mathematics and do not protest.

Before darkness falls, the royal boat and the long line of boats traveling with it are maneuvered into a quiet cove for the night. Lamps are lit. Baskets of prepared food are hauled by ropes and pulleys from the kitchen boat to the serving pantry next to the royal dining hall, and Demetrius seizes another chance to improve my mind.

"The compound pulley was invented by Archimedes of Syracuse, the greatest mathematician who ever lived, and a Greek!"

my tutor informs me. "Have I not been telling you, Cleopatra? With one hand and a compound pulley, he once moved an entire ship, loaded with men and armaments. Tomorrow you will make a drawing of a pulley to show how it works." Then Demetrius adds somberly, "Archimedes was killed by Roman soldiers during the battle of Syracuse, even though their general had given orders that the great genius must be spared. Another incident showing that Romans cannot be trusted."

But Father must surely trust them, I think to myself. If he did not, he would not have promised to give them so much of Egypt's treasure—would he?

I have begun to be concerned about my father's decisions. We are traveling in great luxury, but already I have seen signs of the poverty in which many of our people live. Does Father give any thought to them? Is he worried? It would be unthinkable for a daughter to question her father's authority, and even asking Demetrius for an opinion was unseemly.

And so I keep my thoughts, as well as my questions, to myself.

Chapter 8

PROMISE AND WARNING

In the evening of the first day as the royal boat drifts at anchor in the quiet cove, we feast on roast duck with crackling brown skin, rice from the Orient fragrant with spices, custard sweetened with honey, and fruit so full of juice that it drips down my chin. As he often does, my father waves his hands to dismiss the musicians and reaches for his flute. Tonight he is playing two short *auloi* at once. He dances as he plays, eyes closed, as though he is in a trance.

Most of the guests ignore him, but one who does not is a man named Seleucus. I cannot imagine why my father has invited him on this journey. Seleucus is Syrian and claims to be from a royal family, but he is extremely crude. Behind his back, people call him Cybiosactes, "Saltfish Monger," hardly a flattering epithet. He was given the name for his offensive odor—probably he does not bathe. His voice is loud. "Play on,

Auletes!" he shouts. Worse, he has a way of pressing himself up against any woman who happens to catch his eye. I am too young for him to bother—thank the gods!—but I have heard rumors that he wants to marry one of my sisters, whichever one is likely to succeed Father and become Queen of Egypt. It makes me laugh to think that Tryphaena or Berenike could end up as the wife of this smelly oaf!

The noblemen and their wives begin to drift away, my sisters disappear, and even the repellent Seleucus takes himself off. Father does not seem to mind. He plays not for their enjoyment but for his own. At first his tunes are lively; then, as the night wears on, the music becomes melancholy and subdued.

There is a sharp chill in the river air, but I stay on deck, listening. Monifa brings a fine woolen robe and drapes it around my shoulders, whispering as she does, "Come to bed, Cleopatra."

"I'll come later," I murmur. "I want to stay here with Father."

The torches have burned low. Most of the light comes now from a nearly full moon. My father stops playing and leans on the boat rail, staring down at the silvery light shimmering on the black water. The sails are furled, and the wind moans softly in the ropes that hold them. The waters of the Canopus lap at the sides of the boat. Wrapped in my woolen robe, I go to stand close beside my father. He sighs and puts his arm around me.

"Well, daughter," he says, squeezing my shoulder.

"Well, Father," I reply, playfully mimicking his tone. We often start our conversations that way, and it usually makes him smile. This time it does not. "You seem troubled, Father," I say.

"You've observed correctly, Cleopatra." He lets go of me and grips the boat rail with both hands. "I'll tell you why. Antiochus has warned me that the agreement I made with the Romans is arousing anger among the people. Many of my subjects resent the enormous amount of money I promised the triumvirate to keep them from interfering in Egypt. They claim that I burdened them with ruinous taxes in order to stay in power."

Can they be right? I wonder, but quickly push the thought out of my mind. I dare not question my father's decision. *He has his reasons*, I tell myself, and wait for him to continue.

"What I have done is for the good of Egypt!" he declares. "I have ruled this country for more than twenty-three years, and I believe that in time most Egyptians will see the wisdom of my decision. I have undertaken this journey to greet the people of the Nile Valley and reassure them that I have acted in their best interests. By the time we return to Alexandria, we will have learned if I have fallen into disfavor."

"But you are their pharaoh!" I exclaim. "Your subjects have to accept your decision."

"Correct again, daughter. It is not necessary to have their approval, or their love. Not all pharaohs are beloved," he adds thoughtfully. "People who hate you usually find a way to undermine what you want to do. And sometimes to get rid of you entirely."

"I understand," I say, thinking of Tryphaena and Berenike. But is he also thinking of them? Is he aware of their selfish ambitions? Or are there others who want to see him stripped of his crown?

"I'm not sure you do understand, Cleopatra." Father turns and takes my face in his hands so that I am forced to look into his eyes. "I'm not sure you realize yet that my wish is for *you* to rule Egypt someday, and that burden—and the power—will then become yours."

I stare at him in disbelief. "But that is impossible! My sisters are next in line!"

"True, they are—and they make it clear that they believe one of them will be queen and that they are prepared to challenge my choice. But the gods have their own plans for us. I certainly never expected to become pharaoh. You are in your eleventh year, Cleopatra. It's time for you to hear this story." He pauses, gazing out into the darkness. Neither of us speaks. At last he breaks the silence. "The Ptolemies have a history of bloodshed. I was not even in line to become pharaoh. My brother and I were living in Syria when our cousin, Ptolemy XI, strangled his new wife only three weeks after their marriage. This so infuriated the citizens of Alexandria that they fell upon him, dragged him off, and stabbed him to death. After these two murders, the people turned to me, the natural son of Ptolemy IX, and chose me as their next pharaoh. My brother was given the crown of Cyprus. I was in my thirties, no longer a young man. I was inexperienced as a ruler, but I was not naive—I, too, could be killed at any time. I saw immediately that, if I were to survive, I could trust no one ever again. Believe me, Cleopatra, that is a lonely fate for any ruler."

I listen to his story, astonished by what my father is telling me.

"It's a brutal world, my girl," Father concludes. "I don't believe in shielding you from the truth. If you are to rule one day, as I desire, you must learn now to be watchful. *Of everyone*," he adds, and I believe I understand: He means for me to keep a sharp eye on Tryphaena and Berenike. He is aware of their ambitions.

He bids me good night and places a kiss on my forehead. I bow low and reach out to touch his feet before he dismisses me.

I hurry off to my quarters, where Irisi is waiting to undress me. I hope she is too sleepy to notice my agitation, for my mind is reeling from the conversation I have just had.

My father may face enemies not only among the people he rules, but also among those closest to him. I understand that it can be a mistake to trust the bonds of family for protection. If my sisters believe that Father has chosen me as his heir instead of one of them, they will do whatever it takes to rid themselves of me. Including murder.

Chapter 9

Sais

On the second day, before the chariot of the Sun God Ra ascends above the eastern horizon, the oarsmen tow the royal boat out of the still waters of the cove. We pass stands of papyrus growing lush and thick on every side, leave the Canopus, and make our way through the marshy delta by canal to another branch of the Nile. The sun climbs high. Sweat is pouring from the brows of the oarsmen when we arrive at Sais, a royal city dating back thousands of years to the beginnings of Egyptian civilization. King Ptolemy will make his first official visit to the ancient temple built in honor of Neith, goddess of hunting and mother of the crocodile god.

Father dons the royal kilt and a golden collar heavy with precious stones. He attaches a false beard with leather straps that hook around his ears. "All pharaohs have worn these, and I must as well," he says, tugging at the braided horsehair. "The ancient

Egyptian pharaohs had some strange customs. My advisors tell me it is best to follow them, even though every man I know is clean shaven."

A servant sets the elaborate double crown of Egypt on Father's head. One part is the flat-topped Red Crown; it was the cobra crown of Lower Egypt, the Nile Delta, before the unification of Upper and Lower Egypt some three thousand years ago. It is combined with the vulture crown, the tall White Crown of Upper Egypt, which includes the Nile Valley and the lands south of Memphis all the way to the Nubian Desert.

"A clumsy thing, but impressive, don't you agree?" Father asks. His eyes look watery and bloodshot, as though he had scarcely slept.

A small gilded boat waits to take us ashore. The crocodiles gliding nearby are close enough to touch. Even the boatmen look uneasy. Berenike and Tryphaena are pale with fear and make no attempt to hide it. Arsinoë fiercely clutches her pet monkey and pushes out her lower lip. Father studies his four daughters. "Stay where you are," he growls, and climbs into the boat.

But I am determined to go with him. "I am not afraid," I declare bravely. It is a necessary lie, but I believe that if I do not allow myself to show fear, then the fear will go away. It is also necessary because I want to show that I am not like my fainthearted sisters, their mouths drawn up tight and their hands squeezed in their armpits.

The king gestures to one of the oarsmen, who reaches up and swings me down into the gilded boat. I clasp my hands to still the trembling. As the boat is rowed toward shore, followed by noblemen in other boats, I watch the water uneasily. I do not draw an easy breath until I have stepped onto the carpet spread on the muddy riverbank.

The priests of the temple approach us with measured steps. They are dressed in long linen robes and papyrus sandals, their hair and beards have been plucked, and their heads are oiled. They bow low with arms outstretched to greet King Ptolemy and lead him in a solemn procession toward the temple of Neith. The chief priest conducts a long ceremony with many hymns chanted, prayers recited, and sacred objects handed back and forth, as tambourines thump and jingle. The rest of us wait while the pharaoh disappears into the innermost sanctuary, where he alone presents offerings to the statue of Neith: a slaughtered lamb, a wreath of flowers, a loaf of bread still warm. When Father finally emerges, he looks exhausted, as though he simply wants to have his religious obligations finished and go back to the royal boat to rest.

He stomps over to where I am waiting. "Enough," he grunts. "Return to the boat."

Father decides to remain in Sais for three more days. On the day after his visit to Neith's temple, a delegation paddles out to the royal boat and requests a meeting with their pharaoh. The men own weaving shops where flax is made into fine linen. He agrees to see them, and the men climb aboard. King Ptolemy gives them permission to speak.

I hear only part of what is being said, but dissatisfaction is written clearly on the men's faces. Father listens for a while, but then he grows impatient and sends them away as another delegation arrives. The next day new groups appear, each one repeating the same complaints.

Father's mood has turned dark, and he orders Captain Mshai to leave Sais a day early. "It is just as I said. The people of Sais are angry," he tells me later. "They want relief from their heavy taxes. They say the workers are going hungry." Father rubs his face wearily. "They have not yet heard that things are about to get much worse," he says bluntly. "But there is no course of action for them. I cannot tell them to take their complaints to the Romans who demanded the bribe, or to the moneylender who demands repayment."

This is the first time he has used the word "bribe" instead of "gift." For, a bribe is what it was.

Chapter 10

Pyramids

At dawn on the fifth day of our journey the royal boat pulls away from the shore. Red and yellow sails are let down from the crossbeams, and the north wind fills them. The boats move swiftly toward the place where all seven branches of the Nile come together as one great river with its mysterious origins far to the south. I am idly gazing off toward the vast emptiness of the western desert when an astonishing sight comes into view. Three huge pyramids rise starkly from the plain, the late-afternoon sun glinting off their polished stone surfaces.

My father comes to stand next to me at the rail. "An amazing spectacle, is it not, daughter? The pyramids of Giza, built as tombs by pharaohs of ancient times."

Soon Demetrius joins us. I am content just to stare at these remarkable pyramids, but Demetrius tries to draw Father into a debate about how such an enormous thing could have been built, how the gigantic stones were quarried and moved to the plateau, how they were lifted into place, how many men must have worked on it, how long it must have taken them.

Father brushes my tutor's questions aside. "I really do not care how they were constructed," he says, "so long as my own mortuary temple is built and the proper arrangements made for me for the afterlife. It is not too soon to begin preparations," he adds. Father walks away, hands clasped behind his back, and leaves me to listen to my tutor's theories. I wonder why Father is thinking now of his life after death. Is he not well? He looks tired, his spirits low. The complaints of the linen makers have taken a toll. Or is it more than that? Does he believe his life is threatened?

Arsinoë rescues me, begging me to play a game of Hounds and Jackals. I agree, but my mind is not on the game. I cannot forget the things Father has told me—the enormous debt, the heavy taxes, the rising anger of the people—and I worry how these problems will be resolved. In spite of interruptions from Ako, the monkey, who tries to steal the animal-headed wooden pegs, I play sloppily and still somehow manage to win, though I intended to allow Arsinoë a victory. Her loss makes her unhappy.

"I'm going to find Nebtawi," she says, snatching up the board and the pegs. "He doesn't cheat."

Before nightfall we drop anchor at Memphis, long-ago capital of Lower Egypt before the unification. It is too late to see much of the old city or of Saqqara, the nearby burial grounds. The next morning the rising sun bathes the smaller Saqqara pyramids in a golden light. My sisters are not impressed.

"We wish we were anywhere else," Tryphaena complains. "This place is as dull as death."

"You're right," I tell her. "That's the necropolis, the ancient city of the dead."

Tryphaena glares at me and pulls a sour face. "Very amusing, Cleopatra," she says, but she plainly does not find me amusing at all.

Chapter 11

Dinner Guests

For eight days a steady wind sweeps our boats up the Nile. Farmers leave their fields, weavers and potters desert their workshops, women abandon their chores, and all rush to the riverbank to stare in wonder at the magnificent royal boat as it passes. When they realize that it is their pharaoh, they seem at first to be struck dumb. Then the cheering begins, and the children run along the banks, waving and shouting, trying to keep up with us. Father looks pleased.

He has instructed Captain Mshai to drop anchor wherever there is a major temple. And so we stop often, for there are many gods and many temples to honor them. Mshai, an Egyptian who has spent much of his life on the Nile, allows me to study the charts he has made of the river. I copy his map onto a papyrus scroll and carefully note the names of the temples and any landmarks I observe.

At each stop Father repeats the required ceremonies and makes his offerings. Sometimes I accompany him ashore; sometimes I do not but watch instead from the deck of the royal boat. The priests always greet him with deep reverence, acknowledging their pharaoh as a demigod, the living connection between this world and the afterlife. While Father makes his offering in the temple, the cook and his helpers bargain for food and drink at the market.

After each dutiful visit, Father returns to the boat and yanks off the false beard and the teetering double crown. We always remain at least one night, sometimes two or three in the larger towns. Then the sails are unfurled and we continue on, past the green fields and the mud-hut villages and the men in loincloths who gather on the banks. Later, when the great Sun God Ra begins his descent, the sails are again gathered and the anchor chain rattles for the last time that day.

The noblemen and their wives come aboard the royal boat in the twilight. They arrive dressed in their finest clothes, the women in nearly transparent linen, the young, pretty ones and sometimes the older ones as well leaving their breasts bare. The men wear finely pleated linen kilts, sometimes with shirts, sometimes not, but always displaying their gold collars set with lapis and coral and turquoise. Each tries to outdo the others—except, of course, one must not outdo the king. To make sure this does not happen, the noblemen first send their servants to find out from the king's servants how elaborately turned out King Ptolemy will be that night.

This is one of the parts of the day I look forward to the most. Love of beautiful clothes and jewelry is one thing my sisters and I have in common. We never discuss it, but we compete to see which of us is the best dressed. Tryphaena always overdoes it with too much of everything—too many jewels, too many sashes around her waist and straps on her sandals, cosmetics too thickly applied. Berenike makes it a point to show off her breasts—a good idea, because they are prettier than her face. I do not yet have anything to display, as my sisters like to remind me. It bothers me that I have not yet become a woman. When I mention this to Monifa, she points out that I am just eleven.

"Another year or two," she says. "Your body will know when the time has come."

"But I feel older," I insist. "I should look as old as I feel. Don't you agree?"

Monifa just smiles and does not answer.

Irisi supervises my clothes. "Put on as much jewelry as you like," she tells me, "and if you have chosen two or three of any item, then subtract at least one bracelet, one ring, and one necklace. Dress simply and let your natural beauty shine." Her advice for cosmetics is the same, and for perfumes, too. "You do not want your scent to announce you before you even enter the room," she reminds me, for I do sometimes forget.

The noblewomen who attend our nightly banquets would do well to follow Irisi's rules for simplicity. Most of them do exactly the opposite, and so do my sisters. I am better dressed than either of them.

The same people appear every evening, along with a few local officials who receive a special invitation and arrive in one of the small gilded boats sent to convey them. The guests settle on cushions at one of the low tables in the great dining hall, and servant girls carry in the first of several courses, beginning with bowls of onions and peppers and chickpeas. When we have finished that course, the servants bring the next one, rabbit stew, perhaps, and then bowls of nuts and olives, followed by fish baked in palm leaves or platters of roast goose, depending on what the cooks could procure at the market that day. We cut off mouthfuls with little silver knives and eat with our fingers. Between courses servants pour water over our hands from basins set beneath each table. Honeyed fruits and sweetened cakes arrive at the end of the meal.

As the hours pass, the voices grow louder and the talk looser. I have become skilled at listening in on several conversations at once. Sooner or later Father reaches for his *aulos*, the noblemen and their wives return to their own boats, and the royal boat settles finally into quiet, with only the sound of the gentle lapping of the river. The guests from the town are sometimes left to wonder how they will get back to shore.

"Tell me what the ladies wore tonight," Irisi says as she undresses me, and long after I should be asleep we discuss the noblemen's wives, how they were dressed and how they behaved.

In my opinion they dress well but often behave badly. They are vain and arrogant. Gossip—the crueler the better—is their chief diversion.

Chapter 12

Crocodiles

As the royal boat continues to sail southward, each day is hotter than the one before. It has been more than two weeks on the river. The yearly floods that carry fertile soil to the fields along the Nile subsided months ago, and planting began. Now the new crops of wheat and barley and other grains are ripening in the fields on both banks, east and west. The harvest will soon be under way.

We have tied up our boats near the river that connects the Nile to the great oasis called the Fayum, the most fertile area in all of Egypt, known for its dates and figs as well as its vineyards. The largest city in the region is called Arsinoë. This delights my younger sister until Father begins to tease her.

"The city is now named for your ancestor, Queen Arsinoë II, but its original name was"—he pauses dramatically—"Crocodilopolis! The lake used to be the home to sacred crocodiles worshipped by the ancient Egyptians."

My two older sisters snort with laughter, jeering, "Crocodile! Crocodile!" My younger sister gratifies them by bursting into exasperated tears. Not wanting to make matters worse, I refrain from pointing out that Queen Arsinoë II had her stepson murdered to keep him from inheriting the throne. This was two centuries before the murders that put Father on the throne. What a violent thread runs through our family history!

Father leaves the royal boat to pay his expected visit to the local officials and priests. This time I choose to stay behind. I sit under the awning, practicing my lute. The sun beats down, fiercely hot, and I struggle to keep the instrument in tune. Arsinoë is nearby, playing with Ako.

Earlier in the day the creature sneaked into my quarters and stole a scarab, a carving of a beetle that I believe has hidden powers. This scarab was given to me at my birth, and I love to rub the smooth alabaster between my fingers and feel its warmth. I often wear it on a silk cord around my neck, but now I see the little thief scampering along the deck, the scarab clutched in his wiry fingers, the cord dragging behind him.

"Don't worry, Cleopatra," Arsinoë says. "He'll bring it back when he gets tired of playing with it."

"Best for him if he does," I warn her.

Ako sees me and races off with my scarab. Arsinoë disappears. I put down my lute and chase Ako, but the monkey stays out of my reach, scrambling up the mast and onto the rigging of the sails. Where has Arsinoë gone? Why does she not come for her dreadful little pet?

The monkey leaps onto the railing of the boat, wearing my scarab around his skinny neck. He takes off my scarab and eyes it curiously, puts it in his mouth, and then spits it out again. I have lost all patience. As I lunge for the scarab, Ako slips from his perch and plunges, screeching, into the Nile.

The monkey flails in the water, panic stricken. I am panic stricken as well. I have no idea if monkeys can swim. "Help!" I cry. "Ako fell into the river!"

My cries bring Arsinoë's bodyguard, the eunuch Nebtawi, rushing to the railing. We both look down and see a dark and menacing shape gliding through the water, directly toward the frightened Ako. Without hesitating, Nebtawi vaults over the railing and dives into the water. In a moment he has seized the monkey by the cord around its neck and flings him upward. Even before the sopping-wet monkey lands sprawling on the deck, the gigantic jaws of the crocodile close around Nebtawi's arm. Nebtawi screams and thrashes, and he tries to battle the vicious beast with the terrifying jaws. But a man is no match for a crocodile. The beast drags Nebtawi under as I watch in helpless horror. The thrashing stops. I hear myself screaming. The monkey scrambles away, yanking off the scarab and hurling it at me. A terrible bloom of blood rises to the surface of the water.

I crouch on the deck, staring at the spot where Nebtawi disappeared. I cannot stop screaming. A small crowd clusters by the boat's railing. "What happened?" they ask.

"You must help him!" I cry, and try to explain. "Ako fell in the river, and Nebtawi jumped in to save him. But a crocodile . . ." I am not able to finish. I am sobbing, and I choke on my words.

Arsinoë has learned what occurred, and she begins shrieking. "You made Ako fall into the river, and now Nebtawi is dead! It's your fault, Cleopatra! All your fault!" She is sobbing too, we both are, and nothing anyone does can calm us.

For years Nebtawi has been a good and faithful servant and bodyguard to our family, and now he is dead—all for the sake of the thieving monkey. I have never felt worse. I curl up on my bed for the rest of the day and speak to no one. My head throbs. Then Monifa sits beside me and takes my head in her lap, gently stroking my brow with her cool fingers.

"Nebtawi has begun his cosmic journey," she says soothingly. "Anubis, the jackal-headed god, is with him. When his heart is weighed against the feather of truth by the goddess Maat and proves to be lighter, our friend will be allowed to go to the afterlife that is waiting for him. It is not for us to determine."

But I worry. If the scales tip the other way and his heart is too heavy, then his spirit will be turned over to the monsters of the underworld. I shudder to think of it. He was a young man, and not a rich one, and I doubt that he made preparations for the afterlife. His body is lost forever.

When Father hears about it, he comes to me. "It wasn't your fault, daughter," Father reassures me. "Nebtawi believed it was his duty to save Ako. The scarab amulet surely protected him."

"It protected the monkey, but it did not protect Nebtawi," I say miserably, and I begin to weep again.

My father watches me as I struggle to get my feelings under control. "Cleopatra," he says, "you will one day have to deal with losses far more difficult than this. And you will be blamed for much more."

If Father believes his words will comfort me, he is wrong. But perhaps comfort is not what he intends. If I am truly to follow in his footsteps, I must learn to handle whatever difficulties—and losses—come to me.

Chapter 13

Expecting Trouble

Our journey up the Nile is now in its twenty-seventh day, each day much the same as the one before it. The heat clings to my skin and dries my lips, but after sunset the nights turn cold.

After close to a month on the river, my older sisters complain constantly about nearly everything. Arsinoë grieves for Nebtawi, and to distract her I play countless games of Hounds and Jackals and let her win. Ako, who escaped a horrible end in the jaws of a crocodile, scampers around the boat, bothering everyone, though no one dares object. I am surely not alone in wishing it had been the monkey instead of Nebtawi who was devoured.

I welcome a summons from Demetrius, who is accompanied by Captain Mshai. The three of us watch the farmers at work in their fields. Canals carry water from the river to the crops. A laborer works a shaduf, a pole balanced on a crossbeam with a bucket on one end and a weight on the other. Over and over he fills the bucket, swings the shaduf, and empties the water into the canal.

"Rain seldom falls here. Everything depends on the Nile," Mshai says, calling my attention to a Nilometer, a long flight of steep steps cut into rock on the riverbank. "The markings on the rock show the height of the water during the Inundation. This year the torrential rains in the highlands far to the south were much less than hoped for, and so there is less water in the Nile," he says. "When that happens, the fields dry out too soon, and the crops wither before they can be cut. You can see that the water is low. Farmers again expect a poor harvest."

Demetrius and I exchange glances. This is not what the king wants to hear. I have already seen the worry on his face.

The noblemen and their wives who attend the nightly banquets are not amused when Father decides to play his *aulos* and joins the dancing girls as they perform that evening. After dinner, I overhear the noblemen's wives discussing him as they prepare to leave. "How disgusting!" grumbles one of the usual gossips.

"It is undignified," says another. "Auletes may be the pharaoh, but he behaves like any commoner."

Their remarks anger me. Slowly, very slowly, I stroll close by the women and greet them with the kind of false smile they are used to, letting them know by my smile that I heard every word they said. I see the fear in their eyes when they realize they have been caught speaking badly of the king—and caught by a princess. They are no doubt afraid that I will report their words to

Father and that they will be punished. What if King Ptolemy—Auletes, as they call him disrespectfully—banishes them from his boat, from his banquets?

"I wish you a pleasant evening, my ladies," I say with another false smile, and walk on. In that moment I get a small taste of the power I have over them, and I savor it.

Chapter 14

Dangerous Passage

I have been marking off the days on a shard of pottery: thirty-three days since we left Alexandria. I love the Nile, but I have begun to crave the intellectual life of the city. I miss the busy harbor with ships arriving from distant lands. I miss the great Library with its thousands of papyrus scrolls stacked to the ceiling, and the Museion when the scholars gather to debate.

We stop for a short time at Hermopolis, a city built in ancient times to honor the baboons. Thoth, the Egyptian god of writing and wisdom, often took the form of a baboon, and thousands of these animals once made their home here. Thousands more were mummified and entombed in the catacombs beneath the city. Everywhere huge sandstone carvings of baboons crouch, seeming to stare at me with their glittery eyes. I find them unnerving.

I am relieved when we are once again on the river, but soon I find Tryphaena and Berenike carrying around a baby baboon. Though it is a remarkably ugly creature, they treat it like an infant.

"We've decided to call him Bubu," Tryphaena announces.

"Baboons can be taught to do almost anything," says Berenike. "We're going to teach Bubu to dance."

I can already guess what will happen: My sisters will quickly tire of their new plaything, and poor Bubu will find himself sadly neglected. He will never learn to dance.

We continue past the ruined city of Akhetaton without stopping. The temples and palaces that once occupied a broad plain surrounded by cliffs were abandoned over a thousand years ago, and still no one seems willing to talk about the disgraced pharaoh who built them or even to speak his name. This uneasy silence makes him all the more interesting to me, and I question my tutor relentlessly. "Who was this man, Demetrius? What did he do?"

"King Akhenaten was a heretic," Demetrius says. "He insisted that his people worship just one god, the Sun God Ra. They hated him for it."

That strange idea runs counter to everything our people, Greek and Egyptian, have believed for thousands of years. Ra is the greatest, but there are many gods! What would those gods think—and what would they do—if people singled out just *one* god? Only those people from the East, the Jews, are loyal to a single god. I have met Jews among the scholars at the Museion in Alexandria and admire their intellect, but I have yet to understand their peculiar faith.

On the thirty-ninth day the royal boat passes through a fertile area of luscious gardens thickly planted with date palms and pomegranates. Toward sunset we arrive at the sacred city of Abydos, revered throughout Egypt as the burial place of Osiris, brother-husband of the goddess Isis. The river is crowded with funeral barks carrying coffins of the dead. Everyone who does not have the money to pay for a pyramid wishes to be brought here for burial.

Monifa has often told me the story of Osiris, the god who was murdered by his brother, Seth. Seth dismembered Osiris's body and flung the pieces far and wide over Egypt. After many years of searching, Osiris's sister-wife, Isis, gathered up the pieces and made him whole again. Her magic must have been very powerful, for nine months later she gave birth to Osiris's son, Horus.

Isis is the goddess I most admire and to whom I am devoted. Because I was born on her festival day, she is my patroness, and each morning I leave an offering at her shrine on the deck of the royal boat. The statue in her shrine portrays Isis with a headdress shaped like a throne. Father seems certain that one day I will become pharaoh and sit on the throne of Egypt. I cannot yet see how that will happen or how I am to learn to use my power well. But if it does come to pass that I rule Egypt, I know that Isis will guide me.

"Make me your incarnation, beloved Isis, the human embodiment of all your virtues," I pray, and I leave a flower at her feet.

The royal boat remains moored in Abydos for five days. It is now the second month of Harvest. Many on the boat are restless and eager to push on, but Father seems to be in no hurry. He continues to be welcomed by the priests at every temple he visits, always reassuring them that he supports their plans to build even larger temples. He is not eager to return to Alexandria and the problems waiting for him there. I had hoped that Father would have more time to spend with me on this journey, but he does not. I would rather be alone than in the company of my older sisters.

I keep up my studies with Demetrius, but I think of all the things I would be doing if I were back in Alexandria. I am used to more freedom than I can enjoy aboard the royal boat. I would return to the marketplace or to the great Library and the Museion. Or I might be attending a dance class with the daughters of the noble families who live in the royal quarter. I am told that boys and young men engage in vigorous exercise and gymnastics in their class.

"That sounds so much more interesting than anything we do," I once remarked to Akantha, the niece of Antiochus, one of the girls in the class. "Since high-born women do not dance in public, I see little point in learning these dull routines. I would rather learn the kind of dancing the girls perform at our banquets."

"You *would* want to do something like that, Cleopatra," said Akantha with a disapproving scowl.

She did not come on this journey. On these long, empty days I would welcome even scowling Akantha for company.

Early one morning Captain Mshai prepares to enter a difficult passage on the river. I study his charts and see that the Nile follows a generally straight line flowing north through Egypt to the sea, but now it makes a great eastern loop. Cliffs rear up sharply from the very edge of the water, and I mark them on my map. The captain orders the sails taken in, and the oarsmen get ready to maneuver the royal boat against the current through treacherous waters. Sudden gusts of wind sweep in and threaten to send us careening into one of the sandbars that lurk beneath the dark surface. I ignore the screeching birds that swoop out of holes in the rock cliff and dive at those of us who decide to stay on deck.

For an entire day the boat travels almost directly east before turning to the south. Finally, after another day and another bend, we enter the westward leg as the river turns back on itself. During this challenging stretch, the captain stops only when darkness falls and it is too dangerous to continue. There are no banquets, no music, no dancers. The air fairly hums with tension.

On the third day, just before the king's boat completes the dangerous loop and resumes its southward journey, Demetrius touches my arm and points ahead. "There it is," he says. "Thebes of the Hundred Gates."

The ancient capital of Upper Egypt comes slowly into view, gigantic pylons and towering obelisks silhouetted against the lavender sky. "I have never seen anything like this," I whisper.

"And you likely never will again," Demetrius agrees.

Part III

Upper Egypt

Thebes and Dendara, in my eleventh year

Chapter 15

CHARMION

After sunset on our fiftieth day on the Nile, we finally reach Thebes. The captain ties up the royal boat at the dock illuminated by torches for the pharaoh's arrival. A group of musicians plays with spirit. Everyone is in a good mood, and after being on a boat, even a luxurious one, for almost two months, we are eager to spend time ashore. But the lavender twilight has faded and it is too dark to see much, even with the torches. The king decides that we will stay on the boat until morning and invites the musicians aboard to entertain us.

The next morning the welcoming speeches and ceremonies go on longer than usual. When I become queen, I will order these ceremonies to be much shorter, and I believe everyone will love me for it. Finally, King Ptolemy is escorted in a grand procession to Ipet-Isut, "the biggest religious complex in the whole world," according to Demetrius, who has been stuffing my head with information about this place for days. The construction of Ipet-Isut was begun by a pharaoh who lived fifteen hundred years ago. Since then more than thirty pharaohs have added to it.

"Now they will expect me to contribute another structure," Father says with a grimace.

But I wonder—not for the first time—*How does he plan to pay for it?* Day after day, at every stop the royal boat has made on this journey, the local people sent delegations to complain to the king about their burdensome taxes, pointing out several years of poor harvests. If the farmers have no way to pay these taxes, then where will the money come from to build the new temples Father has promised? And what about the enormous sum of money he owes to the Roman moneylender? I long to ask Father these questions. If I am to become queen, I must understand these things, and I have a mind for them, as my sisters certainly do not. And yet, as the third daughter, and one who is not even yet a woman, I must wait for him to decide to tell me. It is hard for me to keep silent.

The grand procession moves slowly toward Ipet-Isut. Tryphaena and Berenike have made sure they are near the front, and Arsinoë is with them, but I prefer to take a place far to the back, almost at the end. When I think no one will notice, I try to slip away. Unfortunately, Monifa *does* notice and shakes a warning finger. Sometimes she is strict with me and sometimes indulgent. I am never sure which way it will be.

But now, with a complicit smile, she instructs me to put my royal jewelry in her basket so that I will not be recognized as a princess. We follow the grand procession at a little distance and make our way up a broad avenue between a double row of ram-headed sphinxes. The avenue ends at a massive wall supporting gilded poles with streaming scarlet banners. We dawdle and lag behind while the rest of the procession disappears beyond the gate. We are free.

We are staring up at this wall, awestruck by its enormous size, when a young priest, his hairless head glistening with oil, steps forward. "Welcome to the temple of Amun," he says with a bow, and offers to show it to us.

"Do you think he knows who I am?" I whisper to Monifa in Greek. She understands enough to communicate with me.

She shakes her head. That pleases me.

We follow the young priest through the gate in the thick wall—he calls it a pylon, explaining that it represents the horizon—and enter a huge open courtyard filled with gigantic stone columns and colossal statues.

"There is nothing like this in Alexandria," Monifa whispers, squeezing my arm. "These must be the biggest statues in the world!"

I repeat what Demetrius told me: "You will never see anything like this again."

The priest wants to be sure we miss nothing, but the sun is now directly overhead, and Monifa is hot and tired and needs to rest. I suggest that we find the marketplace, and the priest obligingly points the way.

The marketplace is smaller than Alexandria's but just as crowded, and it rings with the sounds of bargaining, arguing, shouts, and laughter. The sun beats down mercilessly. Monifa settles gratefully on a low stone wall and drops a few coins in my hand, for as usual I have none. I hurry off to buy her a fruit drink. We both know that she should be serving me, but I prefer it this way and she allows it. I bring her the drink and a sweet cake and promise to return soon.

"Do not go far, Cleopatra," she warns, the kind of warning she always gives me.

"I won't." It is the kind of promise I rarely keep. "Please don't worry," I add, though I know she will. I know myself, too—how much I enjoy being on my own, away from the royal boat and the confinement of my royal rank.

I wander through the section where shoppers hover over sacks of dried chickpeas and lentils, spices brought overland from the East in donkey trains, jars of oil, heaps of onions, radishes, leeks, and lettuce, baskets of fresh eggs, piles of flatbread, and loaves of several shapes. Pungent smells of cooking drift through the dusty air.

I leave the food booths and stroll over to the vendors of clothing and jewelry. If I had enough money, I would buy a plain dress like the ones worn by local women. My dress of fine pleated linen marks me as a rich man's daughter. I consider trading a little gold ring, the only jewelry I am still wearing, but that would make the vendors suspicious.

Then I recognize a girl kneeling before a large basket of shells under the watchful eye of a barefoot old man in a dirty robe. She is one of the dancers who perform at Father's banquets. She glances up as I approach and leaps to her feet, bowing low. The old man stares at us and then slowly appears to realize that she and I are strangers in Thebes. Though he cannot guess I am the pharaoh's daughter, he nearly topples over in his effort to show his respect.

I acknowledge their greetings and turn to the dancer. "I enjoy myself more if I appear to be like everyone else," I tell her, speaking Egyptian.

She smiles broadly. Her skin is nut brown, and her teeth are even and white. "I understand," she replies in Egyptian. "Unfortunately, mistress, you do not look like everyone else. Anyone can see that you are a princess! May I help you with something? Where are your servants? I thought you never went anywhere without them."

"I'm not supposed to, but Monifa is tired and I persuaded her to let me go for a little while. The problem is that I have no money, so I can't buy anything."

"I have a little money," the girl says. "Do you want some shells? I am buying them to make a hip belt, to wear when I dance. I have some colored beads"—she opens a small bag to show me—"and I can teach you how to make a hip belt for yourself, if you like. It will protect your fertility."

The shell seller looks eagerly from one of us to the other, knowing there is money to be made.

The dancer bargains with the old man to sell her twice as many cowrie shells as she has money to pay for, convincing him without much difficulty that half are for Princess Cleopatra. We walk off together, chatting like old friends, though she continues to address me in a formal manner, as she should.

"My name is Charmion," she says. "It will be my honor to buy us each a cooling drink, and we can sit in the shade of a sycamore and refresh ourselves."

Charmion tells me that she lives with her mother in the royal harem, the place where women dwell. She is twelve, a year older than I am, and has been training as a dancer since early childhood. "My mother is in charge of the king's dancers."

She spreads a cloth on the ground and arranges two rows of cowrie shells. "Let us look at the shells, you decide which ones you want, and I will show you how to make the hip belt." I watch her deftly string the shells on a strand of linen thread, placing a knot and a brightly colored bead between each shell. Her hands are pretty, with long, shapely fingers. She knots a thread at one end and hands it to me.

My fingers are not nearly as clever or as quick, and I must concentrate on not dropping the beads and losing them in the dust. "What I really want," I confide to Charmion as we work, "is to learn your dances. Will you teach me?"

She glances up at me, eyebrows raised. "There are many who would not approve," she says softly. "King Ptolemy, for one. The grand vizier, for another. Almost anyone I can think of."

"I don't care," I reply impatiently. "It's what I want."

Charmion is quiet for a moment, concentrating on the shells. "I can teach you some things, mistress," she says slowly, picking among the glazed beads. "When you are ready, we shall begin your training." She touches her fingertips to her lips, a sign of her promise.

Chapter 16

The Bath

While Monifa and I visited the temple and the marketplace, our servants erected a village of tents near the riverbank. My tent is made of reed mats fastened to a framework of wooden poles. A thick carpet covers the dirt floor. My bed has been moved into the tent, along with the chest holding my dresses and jewels, and I have told Irisi to find me a table and chair so that I can read and write. Nearby is the dining pavilion, a pair of red and yellow striped pennants flying above it. Beyond it, the kitchen tent stands next to a pit for roasting meat. Still farther away are the tents of the servants and workmen.

Late in the afternoon, several girls playing harps usher my sisters and me to a luxurious bath by the river. Small statues of dolphins stand between stone seats arranged in a circle around a mosaic floor. Our servants help us undress. Pipes carry deliciously warm water from a nearby tank, and our servants stand ready with clay jars to pour the water over us. Naked, we step down into the bath.

Berenike stares at my waist. Irisi is also staring. In fact, every eye is on the hip belt I made with Charmion's help.

"What is *that* you're wearing?" Berenike asks.

"It's to protect my fertility," I tell her airily.

She rolls her eyes. Tryphaena stifles a laugh. Arsinoë says, "I want one too!"

"Do tell us about this fertility belt, Cleopatra," Berenike says in the mocking tone she has adopted whenever she speaks to me.

"You don't have any breasts to speak of," says Tryphaena. "You're not even a woman yet. So why are you concerned with your fertility?"

I know that my sisters are taunting me, simply to see me get angry or maybe even cry. But I am determined not to let them have their way. "I will be a woman soon enough," I say with all the confidence I can muster. "And it isn't too soon to think about my fertility. It will be my duty, as it is every queen's, to produce heirs."

I realize, too late, that I have made a mistake. I should never have mentioned a queen's duty. Berenike leaps upon my words, her eyes gleaming like the eyes of a cat about to seize a fish.

"Dear Cleopatra," she purrs, "there is no reason for you to have the least thought about your fertility or the duties of a queen. Should you ever desire to be a bearer of children, I wish you well, of course. But you will never be queen of Egypt! Never!"

Tryphaena rises from the bath. "You're always being praised for your intelligence, Cleopatra," she says, stretching lazily. "I have no idea who puts such stupid ideas into your head, but it would be better for you to rid yourself of such thoughts. They can only bring you harm."

Tryphaena and Berenike exchange a glance that sends a shiver of fear up my spine. Fear is transforming my dislike of my sisters into hatred. And now my sisters have made me furiously angry. I am tempted to reply with Father's words to me on that first night on the river: *My wish is for you to rule Egypt*, but I recognize that doing so would only increase their malevolence. And so, with an effort, I remain silent and close my ears to my older sisters' laughter.

Our servants dry us with soft linen towels and rub our bodies with perfumed oils, and we return to our tents.

I fling myself on my bed and give in to wild tears. Monifa and Irisi try to comfort me, but I refuse to tell them what has upset me, and eventually they leave me alone to exhaust my rage in silence.

Chapter 17

TEMPLES

My anger at my older sisters burns steadily, but I refuse to let it master me. We avoid one another as much as possible. Only Arsinoë notices, or speaks of it.

"You hate them, don't you?" she asks.

"I don't hate them," I tell her. "We disagree, that's all."

"But they hate *you*," she says.

"How do you know that, Arsinoë?" I ask.

"I've heard them say so." She looks away.

Now she has my full attention. "What else do they say?"

"That you want to be queen, but they won't let it happen."

"Anything more?"

Silence.

"Will you tell me if they say anything else?"

"Maybe," she says, and skips away.

I wonder what else she knows, what secrets a nine-year-old

can keep. Is she in league with Tryphaena and Berenike? Does she carry tales to them, as she does to me? I recognize that I must be more watchful of Arsinoë.

We stay in Thebes for several days. By my count, it is now the end of the second month of the journey. Father meets with local leaders, no doubt making all sorts of promises he does not intend to keep. While he is occupied, Demetrius and I explore not only the temple of the creator-god Amun, the main part of Ipet-Isut, but also those parts of the complex dedicated to Amun's wife, the mother-god Mut.

Even Demetrius is not able to explain the many gods and their qualities. I am relieved when my tutor grows weary and is ready to return to the royal tents. As we walk along the riverbank, where it is cooler, Demetrius stops to point across the river to the royal necropolis on the western bank. For almost two thousand years kings and queens and members of the nobility were buried in hidden tombs dug into the limestone. Yet in spite of every precaution, grave robbers found the tombs and stole their treasures. The tombs have been broken into so many times that guards are posted to keep out thieves.

At the foot of a great limestone cliff an eerily deserted temple lies half-buried in drifting sand. It is not like any other temple I have seen and must have been quite beautiful in its time. As the desert sands continue to blow in, it may soon disappear entirely, like a dream.

"The temple of Hatshepsut," Demetrius explains. "She was an amazing queen, though little evidence remains of her rule. Only a few of the scholars at the Museion know anything about her. She dared to rule as pharaoh—she even wore the false beard and the royal kilt. I believe you would find much to admire about her, but you will not see her name on any of the king lists. Her statues were smashed and all representations of her erased, even from the walls of her own temple."

"Someone must have really hated her," I murmur as we walk on.

"Her stepson, probably. She overshadowed him, and he resented her."

"But why?"

Demetrius lifts his shoulders in his familiar gesture. "Power, Cleopatra! Hatshepsut had it, and she was not afraid to use it."

I consider this as my tutor and I make our way back to our tents. I am beginning to understand that whoever has power also has enemies. *Was Hatshepsut ever afraid? Would I have her courage? Because someday soon, I may need it.*

Irisi is waiting for me. "Do you wish to join your sisters at the bath today?" she asks. "I have fresh linens ready for you."

The pleasure of bathing in the lovely warm water is appealing, but the idea of having to listen to the idle chatter of Tryphaena and Berenike and their gibes about my beaded belt ignites my anger all over again.

"No," I tell her. "I want to stay here in the tent and rest." *And avoid my hateful sisters*, but I do not say that.

I lie down on my bed, and Monifa draws the silk curtains. I hear the musicians come to escort my sisters to the bath and Monifa telling them that I am resting. I close my eyes, but they snap open at once when Tryphaena and Berenike rudely open the curtains and, laughing loudly, rush into my tent with Arsinoë just behind them.

"Well, now, what's this? Up, up, dear sister! What will people say if you're not with us at the baths this afternoon?"

"I was out exploring the temples with Demetrius, and I want to rest," I tell them, though they do not deserve an explanation of what I have been doing. "Please, dear sisters, do go on without me."

"It won't be half so amusing if you're not there, Cleopatra. We want to see your fertility belt!" Berenike cries. "Are you wearing it now?" She snatches my coverlet, but I manage to hold on to it.

"We've been thinking that we'd like to have them as well," adds Tryphaena. "Where did you get it? Come, now, Cleopatra, tell us!"

"I don't need to tell you anything!" I am shouting, though I know this is a mistake. I try to lower my voice.

My raised voice summons Monifa, who stares openmouthed at me clutching my coverlet while my sisters try to pull it off. Tryphaena turns on my servant. "What are you gaping at, old woman? Where did our sister get that cowrie-shell belt?" she demands.

"I have no idea, mistress," Monifa murmurs, bowing politely. She is lying, of course, and I am grateful for that. Monifa does not like my sisters any more than I do, but she is a servant and must not allow her feelings to show.

My sisters again exchange the look that I have come to recognize and fear. This time my fear is for Monifa as well as for myself.

Berenike makes a sound of disgust, as though she has tasted something bitter. "I don't know why we even bother with you," she says. "We were simply trying to be friendly, as sisters should."

They leave my tent as rudely as they entered. Monifa makes sure the silk curtains are closed behind them. She looks down at me and lays a cool, soothing hand on my forehead.

"Rest, dear child," she says, and goes away.

It is quiet now. I close my eyes again, and to keep from thinking about my sisters, I let my thoughts drift back to that long-ago and nearly forgotten queen, Hatshepsut.

When I become queen, I will be like Hatshepsut. A real pharaoh! I will not be vain and empty-headed and interested only in luxury, giving orders just to have people obey me. I will be strong and powerful, and I will rule justly and well. I will command the love and respect of my people, and I will . . .

I am drifting off to sleep. But before I do, I realize that I have begun to think in a different way. I no longer think, *If* I should become queen. Now I think, *When* I become queen—no matter what my sisters believe.

Chapter 18

DANCERS

The days drift by, slow as the Nile itself. It is now the third month of Harvest, and we have been in Thebes for twenty-four days. The heat bears down on us. I spend much of the time in my tent, reading and studying. The servants have dampened the reed mats, and the steady breeze from the north blows through the mats and cools my tent. Hardly anyone is stirring, but I am restless, and I decide to borrow one of Irisi's dresses and go looking for Charmion. I have not spoken to her since the day she helped me to make my hip belt, though I see her dancing at the nightly banquets. Sometimes I manage to catch her eye, but she always looks away quickly.

I find the kitchen tent, where the cooks are preparing the evening meal, sweat streaming down their faces, and ask one of the helpers to show me the way to the dancers' quarters. He grunts and points with his chin toward a grove of trees. I am about to rebuke him for his rude response when I realize that he does not know who I am in Irisi's dress, and that pleases me. I walk in the way he pointed until I hear the light tapping of a drum and the jingle of a sistrum and follow the sound to an open space among the trees. Several of the girls lie sprawled on the ground in a patch of shade. Some arch their bodies into graceful backbends, then spring upright again with no effort. The rest are practicing jumps that look complicated and difficult.

They are all naked.

I step back quickly, hoping not to have been noticed, but an elegant dark-skinned woman sees me and holds up her hand. The drummer stops drumming. The dancers halt midstep. Charmion recognizes me and hurries over to where I stand.

"Welcome, mistress," she says, bowing low. "How may we serve you?"

"You promised to teach me to dance," I remind her. "It is my desire to dance with you at the king's banquet." I am only half-joking.

"But you are a royal princess, mistress!" Charmion exclaims, her dark eyes wide. "It would not be seemly for the king's daughter to be seen dancing with us."

"Then I shall wear a disguise. A wig. No one will recognize me." I am beginning to take the idea seriously.

But Charmion bursts out laughing. "Only a fool would not recognize Princess Cleopatra!" The dancers cover their faces with their hands and peer at me from between their fingers.

"I know it is impossible, though it *would* be amusing! And I would enjoy seeing the expression on my sisters' faces! But please—just teach me to dance, and I promise you no one will learn our secret."

Charmion glances at the older woman, who gives the slightest of nods. "First you must meet Lady Amandaris, who is in charge of the dancers. She is my mother."

Lady Amandaris greets me with a warm smile. "We are honored to have you with us and pleased to serve you in whatever way you wish."

It is impossible not to like her at once. Clearly, it is from her that Charmion came by her good looks and graceful manner.

Charmion leads me to the center of the circle. The dancers bow and move aside to make room for me. "First," Charmion says, "you must remove your dress."

I do as she asks.

"Try to imitate exactly what I do," she instructs me. "Start with a simple running step."

The drummer and sistrum player begin a slow, steady beat. The dancers fall into line behind Charmion, and I follow them, walking in time to the rhythm. The tempo increases; I hurry to keep up. Soon we are running. Small hops are added between the running steps. The hops become leaps. We are no longer in a line. The leaping is frenzied. I try to imitate the others as they spin and whirl. What a glorious feeling! Never have I felt so free. The dance classes with Akantha and the other daughters of nobility were nothing like this. But the spinning and whirling make me dizzy. I stumble and collapse into a graceless heap. I feel as though I am still whirling.

Charmion bends over me, frowning with concern. "Are you all right, mistress?"

I sit up, blinking. A furry creature is peering into my face. I stifle a shriek, then I recognize my sisters' baboon, who is wearing a splendid gold collar. Suddenly, Berenike dashes into the midst of the dancers, shouting, "Bubu! Bubu!" For a moment she does not recognize me, just one more naked dancer.

Tryphaena, reaching for her baboon, looks straight at me. Her mouth falls open.

"Cleopatra!" she cries. "What are you doing here? We've been looking for you everywhere! This is hardly the proper place for you. Father would be very displeased." A slow, triumphant smile crosses her face. "I must find some time with him. He'll be most interested to learn how you've chosen to pass your time." She glances at the dancers, adding with a sneer, "And with what sort of people."

I resent her attitude toward the dancers, but, lying naked on the ground, I am in no position to reproach her. "Why are you looking for me?" I ask impatiently.

"Titus has just arrived here," Berenike explains, her eyes bright with excitement. Titus is the nephew of the grand vizier and is also Akantha's brother; the last I saw him he was a gangling youth. "Antiochus sent him with an urgent message for Father. We must leave for Alexandria as soon as we can."

"Come now, Cleopatra," Tryphaena orders in the regal tone she has recently adopted. "But first put on your clothes."

My sisters carry off Bubu, who regards me with a smug expression. I dress hurriedly and run back to my tent, wondering what could have happened to change Father's plans. But I am even more worried about what Father will say if my sisters are as good as their word and inform him that I have been with the dancers. And naked, as well.

Chapter 19

Titus

Father had intended to sail up the Nile to the First Cataract—as far as our boats could travel before boulders blocked the way—with a stop at Hermonthis to venerate Buchis, the sacred bull. This would have extended our journey by at least another thirty days, into a fourth month and maybe even longer. But with the unexpected arrival of Antiochus's nephew Titus, the plan has been abandoned.

"He came in a small, fast boat," Irisi tells me when I return to my tent after my afternoon with Charmion and the other dancers. "His oarsmen have been rowing night and day."

"But why has he come here?" I ask. "What has happened?"

"We know nothing of what is in the grand vizier's message. All we have been told is that the king has ordered Captain Mshai to return immediately to Alexandria."

Whatever news Titus brought is surely not good. Like everyone else, I must wait for an explanation from Father. That evening he orders a fine banquet in honor of Titus's arrival.

Titus is no longer the gangling youth I remember. He has grown tall and broad shouldered with dark, curly hair, a straight nose, and well-muscled thighs. He is very handsome and amiable, and he quickly becomes the center of attention. I am not surprised to observe my older sisters doing everything they can to catch his eye, smiling up at him from beneath their fluttering lashes, inviting him to come and sit by them. But he maintains a very grave and formal manner, and he treats my sisters with great courtesy even as he ignores their invitations. If Titus is wise, he will avoid their little traps.

The banquet is one of the most festive yet. Course after course is served, the musicians and dancers perform. Charmion is careful not to glance in my direction. My father plays his *aulos*. It is as if nothing unusual were happening. Then Father signals for quiet, and everyone leans forward to hear what the king has to say.

"Tomorrow we leave Thebes and return to Alexandria with all speed," he announces. "I have important business to attend to there. By the time the great Ra has begun his climb into the sky, we will be on our way."

His words leave our questions unasked and unanswered.

I am ready to go back to Alexandria, and I think everyone else must feel the same. But this great rush makes me uneasy, because I do not yet know the reason for it. Why is Father being so secretive? I wonder if it has to do with the Romans. Are they demanding more money? Has the general Father mistrusts, Julius Caesar, gone back on his word?

Talk to me, Father, I beg silently. *Explain to me what is happening.*

I stay out on deck until very late, watching the preparations for our departure at sunrise and staying alert for rumors. Maybe Father will come out and speak to me. But the only talk I manage to overhear concerns Titus: My two older sisters are arguing about him.

"I saw the way he looked at me." Tryphaena sighs. "I can see that he finds me very beautiful."

"Beautiful, yes, but he could not help but notice that I have the intelligence to complement my beauty," Berenike retorts.

"Are you saying that Titus finds me stupid?" Tryphaena cries.

Berenike makes a small effort to soothe her. "I'm not saying anything like that. I am only pointing out that Titus is the kind of man who is interested in a woman who has more to her than a pretty face. A woman like me."

"Let us see whom he chooses to sit by at the next banquet," Tryphaena taunts her.

"Surely it will be me," snaps Berenike.

And so it goes, their bickering. Not a word about whatever crisis awaits our father.

Just before sunrise, Captain Mshai orders the crew to cast off, and we leave Thebes behind us. We are going home.

Chapter 20

Shipwreck

The sails are permanently furled, and now we move downriver with the current, against the prevailing winds. We have been away for many days, and I am ready to return to Alexandria. The captain has ordered the master of the oarsmen to drive his men to the limits of their endurance. Instead of the drumbeat that set the rhythm at the beginning of our travels, I hear the crack of the whip. After two days, the royal boat and the fleet of smaller craft traveling with it enter the great eastward loop of the Nile. I choose to stay out on the deck. I enjoy the excitement, and I know I will not have to speak to my sisters, who have taken refuge in their rooms.

Demetrius finds me here. "The river is nearing its lowest point," he says in that familiar lecture tone. "In another month the harvest will be finished. Already the sun is baking the earth and purifying it. Soon the rains will begin far to the south, and the river will swell—all part of the natural rhythm of the Nile. But now, with the low water level, it is a dangerous time on the river. It would be much safer for you to stay in your quarters, Cleopatra."

I murmur some sort of agreement but stay where I am.

The sandbars that were submerged earlier as we journeyed upstream just a month ago are now exposed, and navigating around them proves difficult for a vessel as large as the royal boat.

On the first day, we make good progress through this treacherous area. That pleases Father. But just after sunset on the second day, disaster strikes. Though the sky remains bright, the towering cliffs render the water black and unreadable. Suddenly, a whirlpool snatches one of the small boats accompanying us and sucks it down before anyone even realizes what is happening. A moment later a second boat is drawn into the vortex. The cries of people flung into the roiling waters echo from the cliffs. The other boats struggle fiercely to escape the irresistible pull of the swirling water. How many people are flailing about in the water, screaming for help? How many have already vanished beneath the surface? Are Charmion and Lady Amandaris among them? Who else has been lost? The scene is utterly chaotic, and it is impossible to know.

I scream, "Save them! Save them!" But my words are carried away in the wind.

Then I see Titus vault over the side of the boat and plunge into the water. With great effort he manages to drag two women away from the whirlpool. One slips from his grasp. Three crewmen also jump in to help, but the ferociously whirling and sucking black water quickly overpowers them, and they disappear.

Titus fights his way to two more victims and somehow saves them from drowning. He returns for a third time.

Captain Mshai shouts orders to the oarsmen, who row desperately to maneuver the royal boat to the western shore, and for a time it seems that we have avoided the worst. Then the boat lurches sickeningly, and there is the sound of splintering wood. The boat grinds to a sudden halt, knocking me off my feet, and comes to rest at an odd angle. Father, ashen faced, rushes frantically back and forth across the tilting deck. My older sisters burst out of their rooms. "We're going to die!" they wail. "The boat will sink and we will all drown!" I look at them coldly. My sisters always seem to know how to make things worse.

Father tries to calm them. I am frightened too, but when I realize I have not seen Arsinoë, I hurry to look for her. I find her in her room, hiding her face in the lap of her nurse, Panya. Panya looks too terrified to move. "If Nebtawi were here, he would save us," Arsinöe sobs.

I sit down and put my arm around her. I, too, feel like weeping. "Yes, he would. Now, come with me. Our plight has surely been observed by people on shore, and soon they will come to rescue us. We must be ready." I lead her gently onto the slanting deck, Panya close behind us.

The wreck has happened near the city of Dendara, and the local men, accustomed to the peculiar perils of these waters, row out in their own small boats. Beginning with Father and then my sisters and me and our servants and tutors, they help us climb down into their boats. Nimbly dodging several small but dangerous whirlpools, they ferry us to shore. I find this unexpected journey exciting, but poor Demetrius for once is speechless with fright. The kitchen boat and some of the boats carrying our cooks and other servants have somehow avoided the whirlpools, and Dendarite boatmen guide them to a safe place to stop for the night.

By the light of torches our many servants set to work, creating a new village of tents. Irisi and Monifa improvise a bed for me. Though I am completely exhausted, I cannot rest until I have found the dancers. Not until I have assured myself that Charmion and her mother are safe do I return to my makeshift bed and tumble onto it gratefully.

At sunrise I awaken and hurry to the riverbank. The early rays of the sun strike the royal boat, which is impaled on unseen rocks and leaning precariously. Workmen from Dendara surround it. Father is in their midst, gesturing animatedly. The boat is judged to be badly damaged and in danger of sinking. Captain Mshai worries that materials must be brought from Alexandria. No suitable trees grow in Egypt; the cypress and cedar used to build the hull were originally imported from Lebanon. Throughout the morning there are long discussions with much head shaking. Then the carpenters of Dendara propose dismantling some of the structures on the deck and using the wood to make the necessary repairs.

"It can be done, of course, but it will take time," they inform Captain Mshai, who then informs Father.

I expect him to be upset. He has been in a great rush to return to Alexandria. If he had not been in such a rush, we would not have been pressing on as darkness settled over the Nile. But instead, he seems unperturbed. We are safe for the present, but I worry about what trouble he is both hurrying toward and trying to avoid.

"It is the will of the gods," he says, and calls for a banquet to be prepared to thank the Dendarites for their help and hospitality.

I find the shrine to Isis, taken from the deck of the damaged boat, and leave her an offering of polished stones gathered from the riverbank. *What have the gods willed for me?* I ask her. But she does not answer.

Chapter 21

Repairs

Titus is declared a hero for his quick thinking and his brave leap into the dark and treacherous waters to save several noblemen and their wives. But if he knows why it is important for Father to return at once to Alexandria, he has not told us. I cannot imagine that he does not have some notion of why he was sent on this errand, though he insists he does not.

"My uncle, the grand vizier, gave me an order, and I have obeyed," he has said repeatedly. "I have delivered the coded message to the king."

Titus may not know what is in the coded message from Antiochus, but I am convinced that he is a keen observer and knows more than he is saying. I keep a close eye on him. Early one morning, I find him alone on the riverbank, watching the men at work on the royal boat.

"Greetings, friend Titus!" I call out as I come to stand beside him. "I want to add my words of praise for the courage you showed in the rescue. Weren't you frightened when you jumped into the water?"

"I did not have time to think about it, Princess," he says with a careless shrug. "Many were lost, and I regret that I could not do more to help."

He smiles sadly. *How handsome he is!*

I change the subject to Akantha.

"How is your dear sister?" I ask. "I'm sorry she did not come on this journey. But perhaps it's just as well that she stayed in Alexandria, considering the dangers we have faced."

"I am sure she wishes she were here. Life in Alexandria is not so pleasant for her now. She never leaves the palace quarters. Our parents feel it is too dangerous."

"Too dangerous? Why is that, Titus? What is happening there?"

Titus shakes his head and flashes another of his gleaming smiles. "Cleopatra, I know you take these matters seriously, as young as you are. More seriously than your older sisters! But these are matters for the king."

I am flattered that he sees me as more serious than my sisters. "Titus," I beg him, "please tell me as much as you can."

"Rumors have spread that your father the king is preparing to raise taxes again, to repay the Roman moneylender. The common people are angry."

"Is that why you came, Titus? To warn Father of their anger?"

Titus looks away. "I think it is more than a matter of taxes, Princess Cleopatra. I have already told you more than I should. Now I beg you to excuse me."

He bows and hurries off.

I am worried about Father, but I am also pleased that Titus has confided in me.

Tryphaena and Berenike continue to compete for Titus's attention. "It is easy to see why," Charmion says. "Titus is extremely handsome, and he has shown that he is brave and strong as well."

I agree. "What if he chooses one of my sisters and not the other? What if he chooses both?"

Charmion shakes her head. "Trouble," she says. "Lots of trouble."

But when it becomes clear that we must remain here for many days, Father decides to send Titus back to Alexandria to explain the circumstances of our delay.

That night, we have another banquet in honor of Titus. My sisters are dressed in their finest linen gowns, displaying their bodies as well as their finest jewels. I can scarcely believe it when Tryphaena reaches for a lute and sings a song for him. She does not play well, because she never practices, and her voice is harsh, but that does not stop her. Titus smiles politely, but to me it looks more like a grimace. She sings another song. I wonder if anyone will stop her. Finally, Berenike does. My sisters do not seem to grow more sensible with age.

The next day, Titus leaves in his fast boat—it came through the turbulent water undamaged—and we settle down to wait for the royal boat to be repaired.

Our stay in Dendara lasts much longer than anyone expected—most of all Father. But it is as though he has decided that, whatever the unpleasantness awaiting him in Alexandria, he will enjoy these last days. He orders banquets prepared every evening.

There are somber notes, of course—half a dozen guests and twice that number of servants were lost to drowning in the whirlpool. Their absence is felt but not spoken of.

Day after day, I leave my tent and go down to the riverbank to watch the carpenters of Dendara at work on the royal boat. Ten days have passed. The dancers have found a secluded place to practice, and sometimes I arrange to meet them there. Charmion and her mother assure me that I have a talent for dance.

"You are strong and graceful and quick, and those are the three qualities all dancers must possess," Lady Amandaris tells me, and I treasure her approval. I have always taken it for granted that Demetrius will praise me for my intellectual accomplishments, but I did not expect to earn words of praise for dancing, and I blush and smile, pleased with myself.

Part IV

Into Exile

Alexandria, in my eleventh year

Chapter 22

Return

After nineteen days of labor, often by torchlight far into the night, the damaged portion of the royal boat has been rebuilt. Captain Mshai invites us to inspect it. He seems very nervous. He has apologized over and over to Father. I do not believe he could have avoided the whirlpool, though many—including my sisters—say he should not have attempted to navigate the difficult passage so late in the day.

"He caused the deaths of several high-ranking people," Berenike says. "His life should not be spared. He must first guide the boat back to Alexandria and then be put to death."

"I thought you liked Captain Mshai," I reminded her. "He taught us to sail when we were small."

"That has nothing to do with it," she says coldly.

Perhaps she is right. But her harshness shocks me.

The jagged gash in the hull has been repaired, and the elegant palace on the deck rebuilt in even finer style with material donated by a wealthy Dendara merchant. The whole city turns out to celebrate the achievement. Father makes a grand promise: "In payment for what you have done," he tells the smiling local governor and the throng of officials and townspeople, "I will build a magnificent temple here in honor of Hathor."

Hathor, daughter of Isis and Osiris, is the favorite goddess of the Dendarites. She is worshipped as the goddess of love and pleasure and so, not surprisingly, she is also the favorite of my sister Tryphaena. In her human form, Hathor wears the horns of a cow and a sun disk on her head. On one of her feast days, her statue is carried to the roof of Dendara's old temple, where she receives new energy from the sun. It happens that this is also Tryphaena's birth anniversary. My oldest sister is now seventeen, and she has persuaded Father to celebrate this as well.

Father's announcement is greeted by roaring cheers. The celebration goes on all night, and Tryphaena has made herself the center of attention while Berenike sulks and plots her own birth celebration. She has already declared it will be even grander and more elaborate.

Later, when the feasting and music are over and we are alone, Father says, "Someday, Cleopatra, you will have a son and you will bring him here. Together you will make your offerings to Hathor."

I bow and touch his feet and thank him for his generosity, but I wonder if such a temple will ever be built.

Once again we are on our way. Once again the peasants in the fields stop their work to watch the brilliant procession of boats passing by them like an exotic dream. But there are no more visits to temples, no more sacrifices of freshly slain sheep, no more long ceremonies. We stop every evening before sunset. Now we are truly going home.

As the king's boat enters the Nile Delta and begins to work its way through the canals to the Canopic branch and Alexandria, Father dispatches a messenger to let Antiochus know we are about to enter Lake Mareotis, back where we began. Our journey has taken us four months and thirteen days.

We arrive in Alexandria at the start of the five-day festival at the Opening of the Year. This marks the beginning of Year 24 of the reign of King Ptolemy XII. The festival is timed to the rising of Sirius, the Nile Star, signaling the start of the Inundation and one of the longest days of the year. Though the hour is late, twilight lingers. Torches are just being lit. A crowd has gathered along the lakeshore by the royal dock, and at first I assume they have turned out to celebrate our return. But the mood here is anything but festive. There is no cheering, no musicians are playing, no groups of children carry flowers, only complete silence and sullen staring. If Father notices—How can he not?—he says nothing. I feel uneasy, and my stomach tightens and churns. Monifa reaches for my hand and squeezes it.

The grand vizier and a handful of palace officials wait on the dock, all wearing somber expressions. Guards stand ready to escort us to the royal palace. Antiochus steps forward, bowing low. The king orders him to speak. I can feel the tension, and I wait anxiously to hear what he has to say.

He salutes the king and clears his throat. "It is my solemn duty to inform you, my lord, that your brother, King Ptolemy of Cyprus, is dead," the grand vizier announces in a loud voice.

My father hardly reacts to this news. I suspect that he already knew, that it was in the coded message delivered by Titus. "By what means is my brother dead?" he asks. I believe he knows that, too.

"By his own hand, my lord," the grand vizier replies.

Father's brother was made king of Cyprus at the same time my father was made king of Egypt. I never met my uncle, and I have rarely heard Father speak of him. I sense that the crowd is deeply disturbed. But why? Has the death of this faraway king had consequences that I cannot yet imagine?

Father bribed the Romans to let him keep the throne of Egypt. But, Antiochus explains, the triumvirate moved to annex Cyprus as a possession, claiming that this large island to the north actually belongs to Rome. The triumvirate offered my uncle a position as high priest in a remote Cypriot city if he would agree to relinquish the crown. "Ptolemy of Cyprus declined their offer, claiming it disrespected him," says Antiochus gravely. "Instead, he swallowed poison."

My father listens to this explanation in silence. "Do the people of Alexandria know all this?" he asks.

"They do, my lord, and they are very angry. They cannot understand why you did nothing to help your brother."

"Me?" Father demands. His voice is shaking, and he has gone very pale. "What did they expect *me* to do? Was it not up to my brother to keep his crown on his own head? I can barely hold on to power in Egypt, let alone take up for my feckless brother in Cyprus!"

"The people do not see it that way, my lord. This only feeds the anger that has smoldered since you left on your journey months ago and they learned about the latest increase in their taxes. They burn with resentment that you, your daughters, and your friends enjoy every luxury while they, the common people, suffer great privation. They demand that you return and assume the responsibilities of ruling." He adds somberly, "Your people are blinded by their anger, and their anger is turning to violence."

"My people!" he sneers. "My people can throw themselves into the sea if they do not like it!"

With those bitter words, Father storms off the royal boat, climbs into a waiting chair, and orders the bearers to carry him to the palace. The bearers pick up the chair and take off at a run. My sisters and I look at one another, shocked by what we have just seen and heard. Here, for the first time, I sense that Father's power has begun to slip away like sand through his fingers. I believe that even my sisters sense it too.

"I think our dear father is facing a difficult time," Berenike says. She recovers more quickly than the rest of us and commandeers another gilded chair and climbs in, clutching Bubu. Tryphaena crowds in beside her, though the chair is not built to carry two. With a dazed expression, Arsinoë watches them leave without her and bursts into tears. "What about me?" she wails, but I do not expect our sisters to be concerned about us. They have not cared in the past—why would they change their behavior now?

Crowds of people, their faces twisted with rage, surge around us, rushing away from the lake toward the royal quarter. Demetrius, Irisi, Monifa, and our other servants have been swept off in the confusion, leaving us utterly alone. I seize Arsinoë by the hand and pull her away from the tumult.

"I know these streets well," I assure her. "We'll take the long way around and enter the royal quarter by the harbor."

But Arsinoë resists. "Where's Ako? I can't go without Ako!"

"He's probably with Panya. He'll show up eventually. Now we must go," I insist impatiently. "We have no time to waste on your monkey."

Arsinoë whines in protest—"If Nebtawi were here, he'd know what to do!"—but I hush her and hurry my sister through empty streets. Usually, during the festival of the Opening of the Year, these streets would be filled with throngs celebrating the New Year as a time of rebirth and the coming of the floods. But even the Canopic Way is almost deserted. Darkness closes around us. The Pharos lighthouse blazes in the distance, but without the torches that should have been lighted for the celebration, the broad avenue is eerily dark.

When my sister and I reach the harbor, we find an old man and a boy dozing in a small fishing boat. Waking them and addressing them in Egyptian, I ask them to take us to the Royal Harbor, part of Alexandria's Great Harbor. But they are reluctant.

"Order them!" Arsinoë urges. "Tell them who we are!"

"That we are the daughters of the king who has aroused everyone's fury?" I ask. "Better not to tell them anything." I turn to the boatmen. "My sister is frightened," I explain. "I beg you to help us."

Arsinoë's tears and one of her gold rings finally persuade the old man.

Their small boat glides almost soundlessly over the black water. There is no moon. I can scarcely make out my sister's face. No one speaks. I wonder if the others can hear my heart pounding.

The palace is bathed in the light of many torches, and as the boat draws closer, the angry shouting becomes a roar. I point out the little dock at the rear of the compound, where servants keep a few small boats. The boy helps us climb out. The old man eases the boat away from the dock, and they are quickly swallowed up in the darkness. We feel our way cautiously to a narrow door in the outer wall surrounding the palace compound. This door is always guarded. "He'll recognize us and let us in," I tell my sister more confidently than I feel.

The guard is asleep. This makes it easier for us, certainly, but it will also make it easy for anyone to steal in, make his way to the great palace gates, and throw them open to the angry crowd. I shake the guard awake with a warning. "Hold your post!" I order him, and he snaps to attention. Berenike would not hesitate to have him put to death for sleeping on duty.

We circle to the rear of the main palace and cautiously enter through the servants' quarters. The corridors are empty, but I am not sure if this is a good thing or not. Where is everyone? I steer Arsinoë across a deserted courtyard to her quarters. Her nurse, Panya, rushes out to meet her, carrying Ako. There is much weeping as they are reunited. I wish them good night and turn to leave.

"Where are you going, Cleopatra?" Arsinoë asks, clinging to her monkey.

"To bed," I tell her. That is a lie. I am going to the king's palace to find Father. This time, I will not wait for Father to summon me. I must know if he is safe and what he intends to do now.

For perhaps the last time, I forget to worry about my own safety.

Chapter 23

Promise

An angry mob surrounds the king's palace. I skirt the hundreds of fist-waving, shouting people who are demanding that King Ptolemy come out and face them. I seize a chance to slip by the distracted guards and race through darkened corridors to the king's private apartment. Once inside, I find Father huddled with Antiochus and his other advisors, debating what to do. Everyone has a different idea. The men are so deeply involved in their discussion that they do not even notice when I glide in behind a servant. I recognize the girl: She is one of Berenike's servants. I murmur close to her ear, "I will serve them. You may go." I dismiss her, but she hesitates.

"It is all right," I assure her, taking the jar from her hands. "Princess Berenike has asked me to take your place."

That is another lie. Berenike will be furious when she finds out.

I have never served before, but I have watched often enough to know how it is done. Then Antiochus happens to glance my way. At first it seems he cannot believe it is me he sees.

"My lord," he says to my father, interrupting him, "your daughter has joined us."

"My daughter?" The king's head jerks up. All the men turn to stare at me. "Cleopatra! What are you doing here?"

"I have come to serve you, my lord," I reply, and begin to fill the men's goblets.

"You have no business here, daughter," he says. He sounds weary, drained of energy.

"My business is to be sure that you are served by a friend, not by a spy."

"Princess Berenike sent the girl to serve us. All the others have retired for the night."

I say nothing. Let him figure it out for himself.

I carry around a platter of fruit, but I am careful with the wine, adding only a few drops to Father's goblet. He needs to keep his wits about him.

Annoyed, he holds up his goblet. "If you are indeed here to serve us, Cleopatra, then be kind enough to fill my goblet. To the brim."

I bow low. "I beg your forgiveness, my lord, but the wine jar appears to be empty."

My third lie. I think he knows it, and I am a little afraid he will be angry and send me away to bring another jar. Father reluctantly sets down his empty goblet, and the men resume their discussion.

Suddenly, he rises. "I have made my decision. For the sake of Egypt I shall go into exile. I shall leave as soon as my ships are made ready and provisioned." The men begin to talk loudly, all at once. Father pounds his fist on the table, and his empty goblet clatters. "I, Ptolemy XII, king of Egypt, have spoken! Antiochus, summon the commander of my ocean fleet."

His decision stuns me. If his advisors are surprised, they hide it well. Maybe it is what they have urged him to do. The men stand, bow low with hands outstretched to their pharaoh, and leave the hall in silence. I remain still as a statue, unable to move, though my mind is reeling. My father turns to me. His face is lined and haggard, and he looks much older than his fifty-nine years. I long to throw my arms around him and beg him not to leave, but I do not. It has not been our way to express our deepest feelings so openly.

"So, daughter, it seems we must again say good-bye. It saddens me to leave you, but I have no other choice. I am sure you understand that."

No, I do not understand! I choke back the words. Tears well up in my eyes, but I control the urge to weep. "Where will you go, Father?" I ask him. I cannot stop the trembling in my voice.

"To Rome," he says. "Perhaps my friends there will help me again."

Friends? I am doubtful of the friendship of those Romans. "Will you be gone long?" *And what will I do without you here to guide and protect me?* That question remains unasked.

He gazes at me for a moment. "It may be for a very long time," he says. "I don't know. But I must leave at once. It's not safe for me to sleep in the palace tonight." He takes my face in both his hands and gently tips my head so that I must look at him and his tired, bloodshot eyes.

Take me with you, Father! I cry silently. *Do not leave me here alone with my sisters!* But he does not hear my unspoken pleas.

"Listen to me, Cleopatra. While I'm away, I want you to visit the tomb of our ancestor Alexander the Great and pray for guidance. I will return, if the gods are willing. Hear me, daughter! I promise you this on my sacred word: When I do return, you and I will rule Egypt together."

Have I heard him correctly? He wants me to be the queen by his side? This is a surprise to me, and nothing he has said before has prepared me. Something has surely changed. But what if he does not return? What am *I* to do then? I open my mouth to ask the questions that are already burning. But he shakes his head. "Later, Cleopatra. Later there will be time." He embraces me, pressing me to his chest. I cling to him tightly. Neither of us speaks. Then abruptly he turns away, and he is gone.

Now that I am alone, I begin to weep. Then I remember his words and repeat them silently, over and over: *You and I will rule Egypt together.* I wipe away my tears, lift my head, and brace myself for whatever lies ahead, as a queen must do.

Chapter 24

Announcement

For two days I hear nothing more about Father. The crowds have dispersed, and an uneasy silence lies over the city. Then Demetrius comes to my quarters. "I swore my loyalty to King Ptolemy XII, pharaoh of Upper and Lower Egypt," he says, anxiously rubbing his bald head, "and I promised your father that I would do everything possible to help you."

Nice words, but we both know that even the most loyal tutor has no power. "Where *is* my father?" I ask him. "Is he in Alexandria? Can I see him?"

"I believe that he spent two nights in the lighthouse, in disguise, while his ships were being readied for a sea voyage. The royal fleet sailed today at dawn. That is all I know, Cleopatra."

"My sisters—have you talked with them?"

"Your sisters do not wish to talk with me. That has not changed." He hesitates. "If I can be of any assistance—"

I cut him off, perhaps rudely, and dismiss him.

With Father no longer in Alexandria, I am deeply worried about what will happen. Who will rule Egypt in his place? When King Ptolemy set out on his first voyage to Rome two years ago, he left his grand vizier, Antiochus, to make the administrative decisions. But I have not seen Antiochus since the night we returned from the Nile journey. Did Antiochus accompany Father into exile, or is he in hiding somewhere near here? Who is in charge now? Who will rule?

My sisters have no doubt already made that decision, without consulting me. Before he left, Father told me that he and I would rule together when he returns. But what did he tell *them*? If he told them this is what he plans, then I am in more danger than I have ever been. I am always in danger from those two!

Or did he tell them they should rule in his absence? Or did he choose one or the other to rule? Or put Antiochus in charge? If only Father had told me what to do in the meantime and what provisions he made for his wishes to be carried out! And the one question I must banish from my thoughts: *What if Father never returns?*

As it is, I have absolutely no one to trust, no one I can go to for advice—not Antiochus, or any of the other ministers. The last people in the world I can talk to now are my two older sisters. I hate them, and they hate me. Perhaps they hate each other. If they do, they will destroy each other.

In the meantime, the less I see of Tryphaena and Berenike, the better. The more I can avoid those two and stay out of their sight, the safer I will be.

Irisi and Monifa insist that we must stay quietly in my palace until the situation becomes clearer. "We do not know who are our friends," Monifa frets, "and who have become our enemies." My two servants mistrust the dishes prepared in the palace kitchens, and they decide to take turns going out to the marketplace to purchase food and prepare it themselves.

Irisi returns with a loaf of coarse bread, a bunch of onions, and a pot of cooked lentils. "There is great unrest everywhere," she reports, laying out our simple meal. "And I can tell you that leaving the palace is much easier than getting back in. The guards have been replaced, and these new men do not recognize me."

"But who ordered the guards replaced?" I ask. Irisi does not know.

I would like to take a turn in the market as well. I might learn the answers to my questions. But Monifa insists I must not go out, arguing that it is too dangerous. For once I pay attention to her warnings. I, too, am apprehensive, but I believe the dangers are greater inside the palace than anywhere else.

I feel like a prisoner. The walls seem to close in around me. When I can bear it no longer, I decide to obey Father—and disobey Monifa—to visit the tomb of Alexander the Great. It may be the one place in my city where I can find strength in these difficult days.

As Monifa said, leaving the palace is simple. The streets are crowded, as always, and I can feel the tension in the air; ordinary conversations sound more like arguments. I avoid the marketplace and follow side streets until at last I am walking among the graceful columns of Alexander's tomb. Guards stand motionless, following me with their eyes. In the peaceful silence of the tomb, I kneel beside the sarcophagus. Alexander's coffin was originally wrought entirely of gold, but I once heard that my grandfather ordered it melted down to pay his soldiers. Have my people always had to deal with dire financial problems?

The translucent alabaster coffin that replaced the original is splendid in its own way. The mummy, covered with a thin sheath of beaten gold, lies bathed in pearly light. I have heard it said that Alexander was as beautiful in death as he was in life. I wish I had known him, asked him questions, listened to his answers. How would this brilliant leader advise me now?

Every ruler of Egypt has had to meet challenges, going back thousands of years to the pharaohs who ruled Egypt long before the arrival of Alexander—my favorite, Hatshepsut, among them. I understand that I am one more in the long line that came after him. I must believe that one day I, too, shall rule, just as Father promised. Someday, I would make Egypt a great country, her people prosperous and proud.

Feeling strengthened, I rise and hurry back to my palace. Then I must argue my way past the guard, who does not believe I am who I say I am until Monifa comes out to rescue me. And now she is angry with me too, even when I tell her that I was obeying Father's order.

Four more days have passed since King Ptolemy went into exile, and I receive a surprise visit from Antiochus. I had thought he left with Father. "Princess Cleopatra," he says, bowing—but not quite low enough—"I bring you a message from your devoted sisters, Princess Tryphaena and Princess Berenike. They say that they have not seen you recently, and they are greatly concerned for your well-being."

I do not trust this man, and I doubt that my sisters are

"devoted" or worried in the least about my well-being, any more than I am concerned about theirs. They are no doubt pleased that Father is gone and they are free to plot their own path to power. But the grand vizier and I must play out our little scene. "Please tell my dear sisters that I am quite well and thank them for their concern."

"Your sisters wish you to attend a grand banquet tomorrow night in the great hall of the king's palace. At that time they will make an announcement of great importance."

This is not an invitation I can refuse. It is more like a command. That they are holding the banquet in the king's palace and not in their own is ominous. "Convey my thanks to my sisters for the honor, and assure them of my presence."

Antiochus bows and goes away, leaving me with many puzzling questions.

A single day gives me little time to prepare for the banquet. Monifa and Irisi fuss over my dress and hair and jewels. "I must not appear to outdo my sisters," I remind them. Though they do not say so, I know they are worried about what will occur at the banquet. I am uneasy but determined not to show my true feelings.

The great hall is already filled when I arrive. Two servants escort me to my place near the dais. Arsinoë sits on the opposite side of the hall. I notice that Titus has been given a prominent seat. Musicians herald the entrance of Tryphaena and Berenike, who are elegantly gowned and wearing heavy gold bracelets and collars with precious stones. Berenike leads Bubu, the baboon, on a jeweled leash. I have never seen her appear quite so haughty. Tryphaena, though two years older, cannot quite manage the same proud look. Neither of my sisters glances in my direction. It is as if I do not exist. I do not like being ignored, but I think it might be the best thing—at least for now.

The feasting begins. My sisters entertain their friends as extravagantly as Father ever did, even bringing out the finest wines from the king's private store. No one would guess from this opulent display that Egypt is deeply in debt and that this year, once more, the grain crops failed. The one thing different is that there is no flute player, dancing to his own music. Yet no one speaks of Father's absence. I find the whole affair deeply disturbing.

When the dancers appear, I look for Charmion among them, hoping to find a way to get a message to her, but this seems to be a different group of dancers. It would have been good to have at least one friend nearby. I look over the crowd and do not see a single person with whom I can share my uneasiness.

At the height of the banquet, trumpeters sound the elaborate flourish that proclaims the arrival of the pharaoh. Everyone rises at this signal, and my older sisters begin a majestic promenade through the hall. Antiochus walks ahead of them.

"People of Egypt!" Antiochus calls out in a loud voice, gesturing dramatically. "I present to you your new rulers! Princess Berenike and Princess Tryphaena have bowed to the wishes of King Ptolemy XII to rule jointly and will assume the crowns of Upper and Lower Egypt in a ceremony on the tenth day of the second month of the Inundation."

I can scarcely believe what I am hearing, even though it is exactly what I expected. They are shameless! Rage starts to build inside me. Our father has been gone for only twelve days, and my sisters have already proclaimed themselves rulers in his place. *Is it possible that he actually wishes such a thing?* What did he say to my sisters? I wish more than ever we had had more time to talk before he fled. He might have warned me, prepared me for what was to happen in the meantime.

There is a moment of stunned silence after this announcement, and then the guests begin to applaud—led by Titus—and fall to their knees before their new queens. Arsinoë is on her knees. I kneel as well. I have no choice. What selfish, arrogant, and rather stupid girls they are! I glance around the hall. It seems I am the only one who feels this. How can that be?

Tryphaena is seventeen, Berenike will soon be fifteen, and both are old enough to rule. But I—I am only eleven, and no matter what Father may have planned for my future, I am too young to claim the throne that will one day be mine. Kneeling now before my sisters, I recognize that I am a threat to them. I am sure they recognize it too and will do whatever they can to eliminate that threat.

As the procession completes its circuit of the great hall, I understand that my duty now is to survive.

I will do whatever I must. I owe that much to Father. And to myself.

Chapter 25

Two Queens

The day after my sisters' announcement, Alexandria is in an uproar. The suicide of my uncle, the King of Cyprus, was surely not Father's fault, any more than the poor harvests were his fault. But what are the Egyptians left with, now that he is in exile? Tryphaena and Berenike revel in his absence. Each is surrounded by a group of supporters, and each has her spies. They may call themselves queens and co-rulers, but I know better: They are jealous rivals, and their rivalry grows more bitter every day. The one thing I believe they agree on is their loathing of me. They do not say it, but I can feel it. Better, though, to have them at each other's throats than at mine.

I send my sisters a message, pledging my loyalty and devotion to the reigning queens of Egypt. I do not mean a word of it, and surely they know that, but it is what I am expected to say, what I *must* say.

From then on I am invited—ordered—to attend their banquets, and I plan to be present at every one of them, not because I enjoy them but to observe as much as I can and to listen to as much idle talk as possible.

In particular I will watch Titus. As the nephew of Antiochus, he is in a position to know more than he is saying. He is also the object of a growing rivalry between the two queens, and that could be fatal to one or the other.

Every two or three nights, my sisters host another event, sometimes large parties with the noblemen and their wives, or smaller gatherings with wealthy merchants, lawyers, physicians, scribes, and other professional men among the guests. Even Seleucus, the foul-smelling Syrian called Cybiosactes who accompanied us on Father's Nile journey, is sometimes invited. But regardless of who else is present, Titus is always there. About halfway through the meal during one of the feasts, Titus picks up a harp and begins to sing a song he has composed. The guests halt their conversations to listen, and they applaud warmly, but none more enthusiastically than Tryphaena and Berenike.

Titus usually ignores me, probably regarding me as a child and beneath his notice, though I am nearly twelve, or will be in six months. My sisters continue to openly compete for his attention. Tryphaena sends him delicacies from the royal table, but Berenike outdoes her by offering him a jeweled ring after he dedicates a song to her. I think Tryphaena may be truly in love with him, but Berenike is determined to have him, just to put Tryphaena in her place. Antiochus has no doubt instructed him to be cautious in his attentions to the two queens. What can Titus possibly see in such vain and foolish girls?

I seldom leave the palace now except to visit the great Library of Alexandria. I am not free to wander to the marketplace or anywhere outside the royal quarter. Whatever I do, I try not to attract notice. Irisi and Monifa warn me constantly that everything I want to do puts me at risk.

Demetrius comes to see me nearly every day. I know he is completely loyal, but Demetrius has no interest in politics. He loves history, philosophy, mathematics; power is distant from his mind. He doggedly pursues my studies as though nothing else is happening. When I ask him, "How do you think Tryphaena and Berenike will divide their authority?" he simply lifts his hands and his eyebrows in a helpless gesture, and then he changes the subject, perhaps to a discussion of the use of the inclined plane in the construction of the Great Pyramid.

Dear old Demetrius! I am fond of him, but he is not a real companion, and I am desperate for company besides him and my two servants. Ten days after my visit to Alexander's tomb, I decide to escape again from my loving jailers. I dress in my plainest linen tunic, tie a narrow belt around my waist, strap on sandals, and set off for the royal harem to look for Charmion. I may never master her acrobatic dances, but I can trust her.

The compound is easy to find, a series of low buildings surrounding a courtyard, east of the royal palace. Dozens of women of all ages make their home here. Some of them are distant relatives of my father or my mother, others are women of high status in the community, such as midwives and healers. Some are the king's concubines.

An old woman leaning on a wooden staff regards me with open curiosity. "Whom do you seek, my girl?"

"The dancer Charmion."

The old woman nods and hobbles into one of the low dwellings. Moments later, Charmion appears. She wears a tunic much like mine, though the linen is not as finely woven or as white.

"Mistress Cleopatra!" she exclaims and starts to bow to me, but I stop her.

"Please don't! I would prefer not to have people recognize me."

Charmion leads me into her quarters, which lack the tiled floors and painted walls of wealthy homes but are cool and comfortable. She arranges cushions on a faded carpet, invites me to sit down, and disappears behind a heavy curtain. She returns with her mother, Lady Amandaris, who sets a tray of refreshments on a low table and asks after my well-being. Lady Amandaris is dark-skinned, darker than Charmion, probably from the land of Nubia south of the Great Cataracts, but the two have the same graceful hands and fingers and the same wide smile. Though an older woman, she is really quite beautiful.

Charmion kneels close beside me. "What brings you here, mistress?" Charmion asks after her mother has left us alone.

"I need someone to talk to," I tell her, and pick at the tangled fringe thread on the worn carpet. "I'm sure you know that my father fled into exile twelve days ago and my sisters have taken his place. I'm truly worried about what will happen."

"Yes, I have heard," she says, "and about the crowning, too. Everyone talks about it. I am to dance at the ceremony." We fall silent as Charmion pours us each a cup of sweet juice pressed from grapes. "And you?" she asks. "What about you?"

"For the present I'm just trying to stay out of sight."

"Maybe your sisters will decide to make it a triumvirate, like the Romans," she suggests with a mischievous look. "And you will be the third."

"Very unlikely! My sisters despise me. They don't even try to hide how they feel about me. I think they'd prefer that I disappear." I reach for a fig. "You know about the triumvirate?"

"Just because I am a dancer does not mean I have no knowledge. My mother has spoken of the triumvirs. Now tell me, please—how can I help you?"

"Give me your friendship, Charmion. Tryphaena and Berenike have plenty of supporters. I have none."

"You have my friendship without asking for it, mistress." Charmion places her palms together and bows her head. "My loyalty and my affection."

I look at Charmion's warm, bright smile and reach for her hand. I think of Tryphaena and Berenike, and how since childhood they have made me feel like an outsider, hinting at times that perhaps I am not even our father's true daughter—though I strongly resemble him—and not of royal blood. I have never felt any affection from them—only a growing resentment.

"You are closer to me than my own sisters," I tell her honestly, nearly overcome by a rush of feelings, "and it's my wish that from this moment on you'll address me familiarly, as sisters do."

"I shall try, mistress," she says, her eyes shining with tears. She appears to be as deeply touched as am I.

"No," I tell her firmly, though I, too, am close to weeping. "Say it this way: 'Yes, Cleopatra.'"

"Yes, Cleopatra," she repeats shyly.

"Exactly."

We go on to talk of other things. Charmion mentions Seleucus, the Syrian. "He behaves no better now than he did on the journey," she says, making a face. "He acts in an insulting manner toward the dancing girls. He likes to try to catch hold of our braids. Watch out for him!"

Part V

The Rivals

Alexandria, in my thirteenth year

Chapter 26

Year 2 of the Cleopatras

Father has been in exile now for two years and four months. I record the months and days on a tiny scroll hidden in my chest of jewels. My sisters call this Year 2 of the Cleopatras. Year 24 in the reign of Ptolemy XII ended on the day my sisters had themselves crowned. But to those still loyal to my father, it is Year 26 of King Ptolemy XII.

I was eleven years old when he sailed away for the second time. Now I am thirteen. My studies fill my days—hours spent alone with Demetrius, many more hours at the Library of Alexandria among the scholars. The shelves are piled high with papyrus scrolls, thousands of them. At every table scholars are reading, writing, or conversing in low tones. My love of learning deepens. I, too, enjoy the scholarly life. But I am no longer the girl I was when Father left. I have become a woman. I am stronger and, I think, wiser. I am doubly watchful, less fearful but still wary.

Father's absence remains a raw wound in my heart. Each year on the anniversary of the day he left Alexandria to go into exile, I order my bearers to carry my chair across the long causeway connecting the mainland to the island of Pharos. I climb down by the great lighthouse and gaze out on the vast Mediterranean Sea. Wave after wave pounds the rocky shore, sending up a chilling spray. From this place my father fled from his angry subjects, leaving behind his jealous children. Now these children are two years older and ready to tear each other apart.

I wish desperately that Father would send me a message advising me about what I am to do until he comes back. I have had no such message. No word of any kind. I cannot forget his last words to me: *I promise you this on my sacred word: When I do return, you and I will rule Egypt together.* Determined as I am to survive, I wonder how I can succeed in the midst of such anger and ill will.

My bitterness toward my two sisters grows daily. They strut around wearing the uraeus on their foreheads, the upright cobra made of hammered gold symbolizing their sovereignty and divine right to rule. I go to great lengths to avoid them, but they require my presence at every occasion, no doubt to keep a sharp eye on me. It angers me that both of my sisters have taken the throne name of Cleopatra. "It is Ptolemaic tradition," explains Berenike with her haughty sneer, and I have to admit that much is true.

"You are not the only Cleopatra in the family," adds Tryphaena. "It has been part of our names, too, since we were born. We are older, and we rule." I notice that my sisters now address me in formal speech, ruler to subject.

"We are also more beautiful," Berenike says. She is enjoying this. They are like cats toying with a mouse.

But the mouse turns on them. "I fear that next you will also claim to be more intelligent than I am," I tell them mockingly, "and more learned as well."

"Oh, dear sister," Tryphaena says with a deep yawn. "It takes more than brains to rule well!"

Berenike says lazily, "And there is so much that you do *not* know." She turns to Tryphaena. "Is that not true, Tryphaena?"

They are leading me on, I feel sure, but I foolishly rise to the bait. "I know that I am now of an age to rule," I inform my two sisters through clenched teeth. I do not add, "though not alone," but I recognize immediately that I have made a serious mistake. I should never have brought up the subject, never have reminded them that the thought of ruling has even crossed my mind.

I have infuriated Berenike with these words. She rises, her movements as slow and controlled as a cobra's, and advances toward me, her eyes narrow slits. I glare back at her. I will not let her frighten me.

"Cleopatra," she says in a low, menacing voice, "let us make one thing absolutely clear to you. You will not rule, not even when you are fifteen. You do not have a right to rule. We have mentioned before—and I will bring it up again—there are some doubts as to whether you are of pure royal blood. Everyone knows that Tryphaena and I, and Arsinoë, too, are the daughters of King Ptolemy XII and his wife Cleopatra V. But some doubt has been cast on your parentage." Her voice becomes teasing. "It is possible that *our* father is not *your* father. He was away at the time of—"

"You speak in this insulting manner of our mother!" I interrupt angrily. "Father has never expressed any doubt that I am his child—why, then, should you? I resemble him, everyone says so! And I am his favorite, the one who will one day rule beside him!"

I am aghast at the words that have just slipped out of my mouth. My sisters look surprised as well. For a moment no one says a word. Then Tryphaena says in a falsely syrupy tone, "Oh, *really*, Cleopatra? And how did you come by the notion that you and Father will rule together?"

I back down quickly. "It is my idea," I murmur. "Mine only."

There is a deadly silence, and my sisters exchange a long chilling look.

"Please remember to show the proper respect and address us formally," Berenike says at last in a voice lacking all feeling. "We are the queens now, and you are nothing more than a princess. *As you shall always be*," she adds, emphasizing each word.

Unwilling to provoke them further, I bow low, murmuring, "I shall do as you require, my queens."

"That is better. Much better."

I back away submissively, my face averted, not daring to look them in the eye. If they had any sense of the fury burning in my breast, they would never allow me to walk free.

The two queens do not get along. Tryphaena is idle and wants mostly to be amused. She does nothing for herself and keeps a large number of servants busy responding to her whims. Ambitious Berenike spends her time devising ways to squeeze more funds from the wretchedly poor Egyptians. I suspect that Antiochus does most of the thinking and wields most of the real power, but I also suspect that Berenike may at any time decide he is *too* powerful and rid herself of the grand vizier.

I feel affection and some pity for my younger sister, Arsinoë. She has seemed lost since Nebtawi's cruel death—she misses him far more than she does our father. She has a new tutor-guardian named Ganymede, whom I disliked from the day I met him. He is nothing like Nebtawi; there is no kindness or humor in him, and I do not understand why Antiochus chose him for the post, unless Ganymede is part of some grander scheme. I see Arsinoë mostly at the queens' formal events, since she, too, is required to attend. She spends nearly all her time with Ganymede.

As to the rest of my father's children, I hardly know the two youngest Ptolemies, my little brothers who are brought out only for ceremonial occasions.

Monifa has been with me since I was born, and I love her dearly. Irisi is closer to my age, and I love her, too. But the person to whom I now feel closest and most at ease with is Charmion. If it were not for Charmion, I would feel completely alone. I do fear for her, if the new queens find out about our closeness and want a weapon to use against me. Yet I cannot bring myself to give her up, even for her own sake.

I will soon be fourteen. I have grown taller and my breasts are becoming full and my waist narrow. My hair, once short and curly, has grown long and thick. Tryphaena, who is twenty, and Berenike, eighteen, treat me as though I am still a child—though plainly I am not—or else they pretend to ignore me completely. This angers me, but Charmion reminds me it may be better that they do. "That way, you don't threaten their power."

Charmion is whispering, even though we believe we are safe walking in the city's Jewish quarter, where no one is likely to report us to my sisters. "You must take care not to make them feel that you are a danger to them. Better if you stay out of their way as much as you can. But keep in mind that they no doubt have spies observing everywhere you go and everyone you speak to."

"How long must I continue to do this, Charmion? I'm weary of the game we're playing!" There has been no retaliation following my unwise remarks, though I have expected one.

"Until King Ptolemy returns," she says soothingly. "He will correct it, I feel sure."

"But it has been two and a half years since he left, and Father has sent me no word at all! Sometimes I feel as much anger at him as I do at my sisters. He has left me in danger here. As a daughter I love my father, as a loyal subject I revere him as the rightful king and pharaoh of Egypt, but I am beginning to understand that he has made some grave errors. He has brought our country to the very edge of ruin and left my sisters to ruin it further!"

I stop abruptly, aware that I have spoken words many would consider treason. Charmion is staring at me, openmouthed. Have I driven a wedge between us with my intemperate words?

She lays a hand on my arm. "All the more reason you must attract as little attention as possible. Be careful, dear Cleopatra. I could not bear it if something happened to you!"

Charmion is right. Most days I continue to pass the hours with fidgety old Demetrius. When we are not in the great Library, we move across the agora to the Museion, where almost always someone is making a speech while others impatiently wait to start disagreeing with him. Then everyone leaps into the discussion, which can get quite loud. I enjoy listening to these debates, for these men are among the best educated in the city.

I am required to take my midday meal each day at the royal palace, where palace functionaries and government officials are present. Their discussions often turn into arguments that are also quite loud but much less learned. I eat hastily and in silence, relieved when it ends.

During the meal, Tryphaena and Berenike bicker constantly, their voices rising. Berenike cries, "You are lazy and spoiled and do nothing that is worthwhile!"

Tryphaena shouts back at her, "And you are demanding and selfish and think of no one but yourself!"

They are both correct. I wonder how much longer their idea of joint rule will last. Behind their harsh accusations and cutting words lies their contest for the attention of Titus, the hero of Dendara. It has become obvious from the long, lingering looks they exchange that Tryphaena is indeed in love with Titus, and he with her. Whether they have actually become lovers I cannot say, though Charmion and I suspect they are.

"Of course they are lovers!" Charmion has insisted all along. "I'm sure they've been lovers since soon after we all returned from Thebes. But if you watch closely, Berenike has not yet abandoned her hopes of winning him. She may not truly love him, but she is jealous, and you can be sure she doesn't want Tryphaena to have him."

Sooner or later this situation is certain to reach a crisis, and I am afraid to think what the outcome will be. I cannot imagine that Berenike would cause harm to Tryphaena, but she might decide to create trouble for Titus.

It happens that one day as Demetrius and I are walking back to my palace from the great Library, we encounter Titus and exchange greetings. I make a quick decision. "Demetrius, I have forgotten the papyrus I had intended to bring with me. Please go on without me. I'm sure Titus will agree to accompany me." I smile broadly at Titus. "Won't you, Titus?"

"Of course, my princess," he replies with a correct bow.

Demetrius frowns slightly but shrugs and goes his way. There is no forgotten papyrus, but Titus and I return to the Library and I quickly choose one. As we start back to the palace, our conversation is lively—I inquire about his sister, Akantha—and eventually I mention my own sisters.

"They are rivals, as you surely know," I tell him, my steps slowing. "If you choose one over the other, you could put yourself in harm's way. I tell you this out of true friendship, Titus, and admiration for your courage at Dendara."

We have stopped walking. Titus smiles down at me—he is much taller than I am—and I notice, not for the first time, that his teeth are perfect and white against his tan skin. "Cleopatra, I thank you for your warning. I must tell you that if you were just a year or two older, the rivalry would be three-way, and you would certainly be declared the winner."

Chapter 27

Tryphaena and Titus

Two months pass in an uneasy calm, and I count the days until the Festival of Isis, when I observe the fourteenth anniversary of my birth. Tryphaena and Berenike celebrate the festival, but there is no celebration for me. I continue to keep my distance from my older sisters, but Arsinöe, who is twelve, idolizes them. She is no threat to them, and they fuss over her as though she is another pet. I believe the attention to Arsinoë is designed at least in part to show me that I am of no importance. "That is fortunate for you, Cleopatra," Charmion reminds me. "You are safer."

I prefer to spend my time with Charmion, but we have agreed that she must not come to my palace, where her presence would attract attention. It is easier for me to steal away to the royal harem. Her mother is teaching me the art of cosmetics: how to grind green malachite and blend it with oil for my eyelids, to outline my eyes with kohl, to tint my lips with red ochre.

I have not practiced with Charmion and the other dancers since Father went into exile and my two sisters declared themselves queens. "Why do you want to learn the work of a dancing girl, Cleopatra? You who have everything! The finest food, beautiful dresses and jewels, servants to do whatever you want." Charmion is fixing my hair in a new style, pulling it back in waves and gathering it at the nape of my neck. "Best of all, you can study at the Library and the Museion, and nobody demands to know what you are doing there as they do with a dancing girl."

"Someday I'll lend you one of my white linen dresses, and you can go there with me," I promise her, though I cannot think how I will manage this.

It is as though she can read my thoughts. "I would enjoy that very much," she says. "But I understand that you sometimes make promises that are impossible to keep." She arranges an artful series of little curls across my forehead.

What she says is true, and I look away, unable to meet her eyes. "You're right, Charmion," I admit, and then I change the subject and ask, "What are the latest rumors from the royal court?"

"The grand vizier has been coming to visit my mother, taking advantage of the king's absence. She loathes him. If the king learns of his attentions to Lady Amandaris, Antiochus will no doubt find himself at the bottom of the sea."

"No one would miss him," I tell her, but I do wonder: *Why Father would be so angry? Why would he care if his grand vizier calls on the woman in charge of the dancers?*

On the following afternoon Charmion is waiting for me in the harem, and she seems very agitated. "Have you heard? Queen Tryphaena and Titus have disappeared!" she whispers. "Queen Berenike has forbidden anyone to speak of it, but everyone in the harem is talking about almost nothing else."

I know not a thing about this—no one has brought official or even unofficial word to my palace—and I am shocked.

"Do you think they ran away together?" I ask. This makes no sense to me. Tryphaena might be in love with Titus, but she would surely not give up her position as queen to go off with him. "If they did, Berenike must be furious."

"The women in the harem do not think they have gone voluntarily. They say Berenike forced them to leave."

"But why would she do that? Jealousy?"

"Worse than jealousy! The women believe that Queen Berenike not only sent them away, but that she ordered them both killed. They say that Tryphaena and Titus were sailing on Lake Mareotis on her boat and that Berenike's guards boarded the boat and took it out into the marshes of the delta. No one has seen the boat, or Tryphaena or Titus, since then."

"Berenike had them murdered? Can this be true?"

I stare at her, stunned. Berenike, like Tryphaena, can be cruel, but is she ruthless enough to have done this? I remember the crocodiles with dark bronze backs gliding past the royal boat. I remember how frightened we were when Father went ashore at Sais in a small boat and I forced myself to go with him in spite of my fear, but Tryphaena was terrified and refused. I cannot forget the horrible day that Ako fell into the Nile and Nebtawi jumped into the river to save him. I can still see the huge jaws of the ugly beast dragging him down into the dark water. Surely

Berenike did not send our sister to such a terrible death! But I fear she is capable of it.

I am trembling, and I cannot stop. Charmion's voice reaches me from a great distance. And then I, too, am sinking into blackness.

"Cleopatra!" Lady Amandaris is speaking my name. "Princess Cleopatra!"

I open my eyes to see Charmion's mother bending over me. Charmion kneels beside me, rubbing a cool balm on my wrists. Lady Amandaris holds a cup and urges me to drink. I sip the liquid obediently, though the taste is bitter.

"You fainted," she says. "Mistress, I beg you, say nothing of what my daughter has told you here today. The order has gone out by Queen Berenike's messengers to every quarter of the city. Tryphaena has left Egypt, therefore she is no longer queen, and it is forbidden even to mention her name."

I push myself up from the carpet and struggle to my feet, though I am still trembling. "I must go back to my palace."

Charmion and her mother urge me to rest, to wait until I am feeling stronger, but I insist.

"Be careful, mistress," Lady Amandaris warns me. "We are afraid for your safety."

I embrace them both—the first time I have done this—and hurry away.

I rush past the guards standing stiffly by the entrance to my palace and find Irisi and Monifa wringing their hands, frantic with worry. The rumors have reached them—that Tryphaena and Titus have disappeared, that they are likely dead, that Queen Berenike is responsible.

"The royal messenger was just here," Irisi says. "We are not to speak of Queen Tryphaena."

"It is one thing to issue such an order and quite another to stop people from doing it," I remind them. I think of Hatshepsut, the queen whose image was erased from every building she had constructed, even from the walls of her beautiful temple. But that did not end the talk about her.

Chapter 28

Berenike

In spite of Berenike's edict, rumors of the fate of Tryphaena and Titus grow even more gruesome. Announcements from the palace are now dated YEAR 2 IN THE REIGN OF QUEEN CLEOPATRA BERENIKE. Tryphaena's name is not mentioned.

It is summer again, the season of Inundation, the annual flooding of the Nile. We pretend that everything is normal, though it is not. My nerves are on edge. I have always known that Berenike might choose at any time to eliminate me as well. I sleep little—will one of the queen's guards force his way into my palace at night and stab me in my bed? Fearing poison, I refuse to eat or drink anything unless Monifa prepares it with her own hands.

Then, as expected, I receive a summons from Berenike. I hurry to obey, though I dread it. She no longer lives in the pretty little palace that has been hers since childhood but has taken over the king's palace. The throne room where Father once received important visitors from many countries looks much different now. The walls have been repainted with bright scenes, many showing Queen Berenike making offerings to the gods.

Glittering with jewels, the queen reclines on her new ebony throne. Inlaid with ivory and decorated with gold, the throne is raised on a dais at the end of the great hall, and on either side of it stands a guard dressed in silk, each guard holding a spotted leopard on a leash. The leopards gaze at me coolly with their glowing amber eyes. One of the creatures stretches lazily, the dark spots rippling over his sleek body, and yawns, showing white fangs.

Berenike's lips and nails are tinted with henna, her eyes outlined with kohl. On her forehead is the uraeus, the golden cobra, erect and ready to strike. I glance around cautiously to see who else is present, but except for her two guards with the leopards, we are alone. I bow low and wait silently, my head pounding.

Queen Berenike smiles without warmth. "Welcome, Cleopatra," she says. The flinty edge to her voice makes me increasingly uneasy. She gestures grandly around the vast hall. "How do you like my new throne room? Elegant, is it not?"

I cannot say what I am thinking: *It is not yours. It is Father's.* I force a smile. "It suits you perfectly, my queen." But then I cannot seem to stop myself from asking, "Does Queen Tryphaena have one like it?" I immediately regret my question. Berenike will know it is not innocent, that I have deliberately ignored the edict not to speak Tryphaena's name. But now it is too late to take it back.

Berenike purses her lips. "Interesting that you should ask about her, Cleopatra! In fact, I have not seen our sister for some time. I have been busy overseeing the redecoration of the king's palace, and there is no end to the matters of state that keep me occupied from dawn until dusk, and beyond. One of the reasons I summoned you is to ask if *you* might have seen our sister and her *good friend* Titus." Berenike says "good friend" with peculiar emphasis. "They seem to have vanished. You get out and about so much more than I do, Cleopatra. Visiting the king's harem, and so forth. Naturally, you hear more." One plucked eyebrow is raised questioningly, and she regards me with an eye as coolly menacing as the leopard's.

A prickle of danger runs along my spine like an icy finger. *Why would she think I know the whereabouts of Tryphaena if, as she claims, she does not? I do not believe her. This is all an act, a great lie. And who has been reporting to her about my visits to Charmion? Who are the spies in the king's harem?*

"No, dear sister queen," I answer truthfully, "I know nothing of them."

"What a shame," says the queen coldly. "Do let me know if you hear anything. Her absence worries me deeply."

Queen Berenike dismisses me with a curt nod. I want only to get as far away from her as possible as quickly as possible, but at the last moment she calls me back.

"Cleopatra!"

The leopards are tense, suddenly alert, ready to pounce.

"Yes, my queen?" I am shivering, in spite of the heat, and I am certain the beasts sense my anxiety.

"I am holding an important banquet in three days," she says. "I expect you to be there."

"I am deeply honored, my queen," I reply, and prepare to leave.

"Cleopatra!" Berenike calls after me again. I freeze in place, my heart in my throat. My eyes lock with hers. "I would much prefer you to spend your time with the daughters of noble families," she says. "Not with a common dancer."

How I despise this woman! "As you wish," I mutter, and flee.

Chapter 29

Seleucus

Three days until Queen Berenike's banquet, three days to wonder what she has in store for me. There is still no explanation of Tryphaena's disappearance; she and Titus are not spoken of. And I understand that, for now, it is better for me not to see Charmion.

For months before Tryphaena vanished, there had been fewer large banquets of the kind Father used to hold regularly. As the royal court became divided into opposing factions, Berenike entertained her supporters in one palace, Tryphaena entertained hers in another. I was seldom invited by either, which suited me well. Now I am obliged to attend. Arsinoë is with me, her face flushed with pleasure. Despite the efforts of Monifa and Irisi to calm me, I am apprehensive, my nerves stretched taut.

The banquet is one of the most lavish in years, with whole

roasted oryxes and wine from the vineyards of the Fayum that our father always favored. An air of anticipation hangs over the crowd, and in the midst of the feasting, Queen Berenike calls for silence. She is about to make an announcement. "I have decided to marry!" she proclaims. Everyone gasps, though this was not surprising: Egyptian queens are not expected to reign alone. "I have chosen a fine husband!" she says, laughing loudly. Her guests laugh along with her. I am not amused—only puzzled. "At the end of the banquet, I shall reveal his name!"

Seated beside me, Arsinoë squeaks excitedly, "Who can it be? Do you know, Cleopatra?"

"I have no idea," I tell my little sister. "Be still, and we'll find out soon enough."

If she follows the tradition of the Ptolemies and the pharaohs who ruled before us, she will marry one of our brothers. But Ptolemy XIII is just six years old, Ptolemy XIV not quite five. Knowing Berenike, I am certain she will have none of this tradition. From my place near the dais I search the sea of faces and find no one who seems a likely candidate.

There has been no mention of the disappearance of Tryphaena and Titus. It is as if our sister never existed. Even Antiochus, Titus's uncle, has shown no reaction to his nephew's unexplained absence. *And what about Akantha, sister of Titus—does she not wonder? She was once Berenike's good friend. Is she still? Does she dare ask the queen about Titus?* A part of me still hopes the lovers have somehow reached a place far away where they can be safe. But I know that cannot be so.

The banquet is coming to a close. The dancers have finished their performance—Charmion was not among them—but the trumpets play a flourish and Berenike announces that she will now introduce her future husband.

"Seleucus, Prince of Syria!" she proclaims.

The bridegroom stumbles to his feet, grinning foolishly, and acknowledges the tepid applause of the guests.

"It's that man who smells so bad!" Arsinoë whispers too loudly.

"Hush!" I frown at her. But I cannot imagine what has prompted Berenike to choose Saltfish Monger as her husband. What power can the oafish Seleucus bring to her that Berenike has not already seized for herself?

From that night on, I feel not only the queen's eyes upon me but also the eyes of her numerous unseen spies. I have nothing to hide, nothing to keep from her, with just one exception: Charmion.

Berenike did not actually forbid me to see her, though she made it clear enough that she disapproves of my friendship. *I would much prefer you* were her words, not *I order you.* Still, Charmion and I dare not meet in this poisonous atmosphere where danger lurks in every corner and behind every column. When she dances for the queen's banquets, we resist exchanging so much as a glance. But after Berenike reveals her intention to marry Seleucus, Charmion and I have too much to discuss to wait any longer.

I send her a message asking her to meet me in the zoological garden near the great Library of Alexandria. The royal menagerie was established by the first Ptolemy. Later kings added to the collection, sending out expeditions to distant places to bring back exotic specimens—lions, tigers, an elephant, even a great white bear. I sometimes walk in this garden when I have been studying for many hours. This is where I go now, taking a basket of fruit for the elephant.

At first I do not recognize Charmion. She has dressed in the rough garb of a peasant, her long braid tucked beneath a headcloth, and is busily sweeping the path outside the elephant's cage. The great beast recognizes me and pokes his trunk through the bars.

"There is a small shelter where the tools are kept," Charmion says quietly without looking up from her sweeping. "I will wait for you there." She works her way on down the path while the elephant daintily accepts the figs from my hand. When I am reasonably certain that I am not being watched, I find the shelter. It is dark inside, not even a glimmer of light. I hear Charmion's whisper. "It's all right," she says, and her unseen hand guides me to a crude stone bench. "No one is likely to look for us here."

Before my eyes have adjusted to the darkness, Charmion exclaims, "Queen Berenike cannot be marrying the Saltfish Monger! He smells terrible!"

We continue to speak in whispers. "And his voice! You can hear him bellowing like the sacred Apis bull!"

"Antiochus told my mother that her advisors picked him," Charmion says. "They don't want her to rule alone."

"Three years ago, on our journey up the Nile, there were rumors that this unwashed oaf wanted to marry one of my sisters," I tell her thoughtfully, "but it's hard to believe that Berenike actually agreed to marry him, no matter what her advisors say. Nevertheless, if it will keep Berenike occupied, I give my complete approval to the match," I say to Charmion with mock solemnity.

"Perhaps you could give her some perfumed wax to hold to her nose," Charmion suggests, and I struggle to smother my laughter. Charmion is the only person who can make me laugh like this.

She asks then, as she always does, if I have any news of Father, and I tell her that I have not. I never do. My father does not write to me or send me messages, and I sometimes wonder if he ever thinks of me. Thinking of him now puts an end to my amusement. I realize he may never be able to return, I may never see him again, and our dream of ruling together may be finished.

I play my proper role as princess at the celebration of the queen's marriage, along with Arsinoë and the little Ptolemy princes. Charmion is among the dancers at the banquet. While another musical group is performing for the happy couple and their guests, I slip out and find Charmion. The night is hot, even with the breeze from the sea, and her smooth skin is covered with a light sheen of sweat.

"That idiot!" she mutters, glaring in the direction of my sister's new husband.

"What?" I ask.

"He—he *grabbed* me!" she sputters, and I remember how he behaved toward the women and girls on the Nile boats. "I pray that he does not decide to get himself a handful of *your* tender flesh!"

"Something else to beware of." I sigh. "As if we didn't have enough already."

Eight days later, Seleucus is found dead, strangled with Berenike's necklace. The queen does not deny that she ordered the murder of her husband, whom she describes as coarse and vulgar.

There is no pretense that he "vanished." She does not speak of him again. No one does.

Chapter 30

Archelaus

More than a month has passed since the marriage and the murder of Prince Seleucus. Berenike frightens me more than ever. I avoid her when I can and force a smile when I cannot, but I am never at ease. Sometimes I arrange a stealthy meeting with Charmion, but each time requires us to find a new and secret place, and I am reluctant to put her at risk. I wonder if I will always live in fear. I am growing thin. Sleep does not come easily, though Irisi and Monifa have moved their beds to block my door. There are no limits to what Berenike will do. She is nineteen years old. Where does she find the strength of will for such things?

Then, only months after doing away with the unfortunate Seleucus, Berenike chooses a new husband, Archelaus, son of the king of Pontus in Asia Minor. She arranges another brilliant celebration, and her supporters rejoice, apparently forgetting all about the ill fate of Seleucus. Archelaus is rough and shaggy looking, laughs at his own jokes like a braying donkey, and spends his days out hunting, but he is not boorish like Saltfish Monger. His first official act as king is to banish Bubu. Archelaus objected to the baboon's presence in his bedroom. I applaud his decision. I think it might even be possible to like this man, and I hope that Queen Berenike likes him well enough not to have him murdered like his predecessor. One can never be sure.

I understand why Berenike decided to marry Archelaus, but I cannot begin to understand why Archelaus agreed to marry Berenike. Does he worry, as I do, that each meal might be his last, or that he will go to sleep one night and fail to wake up the next morning?

But already the queen has a problem. By the time I mark the fifteenth anniversary of my birth, word has reached Rome of events in Alexandria: that Tryphaena and Titus have ceased to exist, that Seleucus is dead, and, most seriously in the view of the Roman triumvirate, that Berenike has married Archelaus without consulting them. Rumors again swirl through the royal quarter. Even Demetrius, who usually ignores political matters, has talked with his friend the philosopher Dion of Alexandria. I persuade my tutor to tell me what he knows.

"Queen Berenike is sending Dion as ambassador to Rome with a delegation of a hundred men," he says. "Their mission is to persuade the triumvirate that all Berenike has done is for the good of Egypt."

"Does Father know about this?" I ask him. "The two murders—three, counting Titus—and the new husband?"

"Most certainly King Ptolemy has been informed."

"What will happen now?"

"We must wait and see. The king is in exile in Rome. Even if he knows exactly what occurred, he can do nothing."

This is far from reassuring. There is not one powerful person on my side.

And so we wait, and what we learn before a new season begins is that Dion of Alexandria is dead, murdered on the orders of my father. Likewise, many members of the delegation, those who were not bribed or somehow threatened into silence, have been killed. Hardly any of Berenike's delegates return alive to Alexandria.

The news appalls me. Why did Father do this? I understand his anger at Berenike, but was it necessary to kill Dion, one of our leading scholars, and so many delegates? My father's actions seem senselessly, terribly cruel. Many other loyal subjects are shocked as well.

"The murders have created a scandal in Rome," the bitter survivors report. "King Ptolemy has been forced to flee once more, this time to the temple of Artemis in Ephesus."

The temple of Artemis is known to be the most sacred place of sanctuary in the world. I know from my study of our maps that Ephesus is a long journey from Rome—and a long way from Alexandria.

"Do you think my father is planning to come home to Egypt?" I ask Demetrius.

My tutor shakes his head and lifts his shoulders in his familiar shrug. "Only the gods can answer that, Cleopatra."

Chapter 31

Bucephala

Many things have changed since my father was forced into exile three and a half years ago. I am fifteen, old enough to rule Egypt alone and capable of ruling well. Only Queen Cleopatra Berenike stands between me and the throne—and she knows that as well as I do. Yet she and her husband, Archelaus, rule without any apparent opposition. Everyone is afraid to anger her. But my time is coming, I feel sure, and so I watch and wait. One day soon Berenike is certain to make a serious mistake. Maybe even a fatal one. And I will be ready.

With Archelaus at her side, Queen Berenike seems less interested in what I do, and I have become bolder. Surely the queen's spies have informed her of my visits to the harem to spend time with Charmion and her mother, but so far she has not interfered.

Charmion humors me with lessons in the dances she performs for royal banquets. "You have a talent for this, Cleopatra," she assures me, "though you will never perform in public."

"Only in private, someday, for your husband," adds Lady Amandaris, who is as wise as she is elegant. "But your truest talent, like your greatest beauty, is in your intelligence and your charm."

"Charm?" I ask her. "I know what intelligence is, but please explain charm to me."

Lady Amandaris is mixing the ingredients for perfumed oils, and she pauses to consider her answer. "To listen well, to think quickly, but to speak with just the right amount of wit, in order to amuse without wounding."

"Unless your intent is to wound," Charmion interrupts.

"But that, you see, is no longer charming," her mother reminds her. She offers me a sample of scented ointment for my hair. "Princess Cleopatra, you will learn in time that you have a wide range of ways of speaking to achieve your desired ends—whether it is one man in particular you wish to charm, a whole army, or an entire nation."

Conversations like this are but one reason I hate to leave the harem to return to my lonely palace, where Monifa and Irisi do what they can to calm my restless spirit. The other reason is that here, with Charmion and Lady Amandaris, I feel that I am loved and accepted for who I am—not as a princess, but as a young woman. *This* is my true family.

With Father far away and her beloved Nebtawi long dead, Arsinoë seems forlorn and often tags along after me. I make it a point to spend more time with her. She is thirteen, no longer a child. It is possible that she will someday become a beauty.

We now have little in common but our blood ties, but I try to change that.

I begin to take Arsinoë with me when I go out to the royal stables. Nebibi, the stable master, helps Arsinoë onto a horse he has chosen for her, just as he used to help me. He shows her how to grip the horse with her knees. But she is stiff and clumsy, and the horse does not respond the way she wants. "Wretched horse!" she cries, pounding its flanks with her heels.

Nebibi brings another horse, but the results are no better. "I would do very well if I had a horse just like Bucephala," she insists, and she whines until I give in and allow her to ride my little mare. Suddenly, she finds that on Bucephala's smooth back she can ride like the wind. Nebibi and I watch in amazement. I am not surprised when Arsinoë decides that she wants Bucephala for her own.

"You must learn to ride your own horse," I tell her. "There is an entire stable of well-trained horses. No doubt you'll soon find one that is perfect for you."

Nebibi leads out one horse after another, but the only one that pleases Arsinöe is my Bucephala. She begs me to give her my mare, but I am unwilling to part with it. Arsinoë is a stubborn, willful girl, and she coaxes, wheedles, bribes, and threatens me whenever she sees me. But I do not give in.

One day I persuade her to accompany me to the great Library. She takes little interest in the papyrus scrolls stacked along each wall as high as the ceiling, but, curiously, she has learned the art of making the papyrus itself. When we return to the palace, she demonstrates for me how it is done, skillfully cutting a thick stalk of papyrus into thin strips, laying out the strips in a crisscross pattern, pounding them into a long, flat sheet, and finally smoothing the sheet with a stone. She becomes so involved in what she is doing that I deceive myself into thinking she has forgotten about Bucephala.

I praise her efforts extravagantly, but nothing I say inspires her to read more than she absolutely must. And she refuses to learn to speak any language other than Greek.

"Ganymede says I don't have to," she says smugly. "Ganymede says Greek is all I will ever need and that all my servants will speak Greek to me. He says it is not a good use of time to learn Egyptian and all those other languages."

My dislike of her tutor has just increased by several degrees. "When Father comes back, he'll be speaking Latin," I tell her. "I'm sure he'd be pleased if you could learn it too."

"Father isn't coming back," she says flatly.

"Who told you that? Ganymede?"

"No—it was Berenike. She says he'll stay in the temple of Artemis in Ephesus for the rest of his life because it's the only place he's safe."

He may be safe in Ephesus, but I know Father, and I know that he will not be content to stay there for long. "Berenike may hope that's true," I say, "but she is wrong."

Arsinoë regards me with narrowed eyes. "I'm going to tell her what you said if you don't give me Bucephala."

"Go ahead and tell her. She knows I'm right." I am not surprised by her scheming.

Arsinoë does not like to be denied. "Then I'll tell her that you go to the harem almost every day to see that dancer and her mother."

She knows that she has hit her mark. Perhaps it does not matter much. Berenike's spies are everywhere. The queen already knows my every move. But I do not want to risk making any sort of difficulty for Charmion and Lady Amandaris.

"You may have Bucephala," I tell Arsinoë. "Treat her well."

I have traded my little mare for the sake of my dear friend and her mother. If anything should happen to Charmion and Lady Amandaris, I would never forgive myself. And I would truly be completely alone.

Chapter 32

THE KING'S RETURN

Father may soon come home.

Rumors fly that King Ptolemy is planning his return to Egypt, as dangerous as that will certainly be—especially for those close to him. Monifa rushes in from the marketplace with the news that Father has bribed the governor of Syria, a Roman province, to send an army into Egypt to put down any resistance to his return. "Ten thousand talents, borrowed once more from a Roman moneylender," Monifa reports. "Everyone is talking about it."

Ten thousand talents! Surely that rumor is false—or at least an exaggeration. How will Father ever pay it back? And what will happen if he does not?

Worse than that: The Syrian soldiers Father has hired will be fighting against his own people, and mine.

I am happy to learn that Father is coming home at last, even at the cost of so much money, but there will certainly be bloodshed, and I worry that my father may be killed in battle. I nervously await word of what is happening and keep watch for any messengers who might arrive at Queen Berenike's palace with news and fail to tell me. But such an important secret cannot be kept long from the marketplace. Soon I learn that the hired Syrian soldiers, led by a Roman officer, have massed outside the walls of Pelusium, an Egyptian seaport on the far eastern edge of the delta.

"No need to be troubled," Demetrius assures me. "Pelusium is strongly fortified. It will successfully resist any attack."

Pelusium seems far away from Alexandria, and for a short time I feel reassured. Perhaps this will all end peacefully, with few lives lost and Father safely home.

But several days later there is more news: Pelusium has fallen. Demetrius was wrong. Now the Syrian soldiers and their Roman officers are on their way to Alexandria.

Queen Berenike's husband, Archelaus, has put himself at the head of the Egyptian army, determined to repel the invaders—invaders sent by my father against his own city! Berenike arranges a banquet as a farewell for Archelaus, and after the usual feasting she makes a grand speech about honor and bravery. A huge crowd gathers the next morning to cheer as Archelaus rides off at the head of an army of foot soldiers and charioteers. Berenike looks on proudly.

Alexandrians wait anxiously for more news. Nerves are on edge in the royal quarter and in the marketplace. I can sense the unease in everyone I speak to. At last a filthy and exhausted runner stumbles into the queen's palace: The Syrian soldiers have reached the gates of our city. King Ptolemy is waiting offshore in his ship for Alexandria to fall to the invaders.

The battle rages. I feel torn. I want Father to be here, to be safe, but at what cost? What will happen next?

I hear a slow, steady drumbeat, and from the roof of my palace, where I pace anxiously with Monifa and Irisi, I see a somber procession making its way toward Queen Berenike's palace. They are bearing a body wrapped in royal robes. For one terrible moment I fear that this is Father's homecoming. Then I recognize the robes. It is Archelaus, killed at the height of battle.

Berenike comes out to meet the procession. She begins to howl, a long wail that sends a shudder through me.

Much later, toward nightfall, Father comes ashore. He moves slowly, as though he is weary, nearly exhausted. But then he straightens his shoulders and quickens his step. He is in charge again. He is our king! Many of his subjects died in the effort to prevent his return, and his welcome is subdued, nothing like his return from Rome a few years earlier. But the city is his once more.

Alert and sleepless, I await his summons. It is long in coming. When he finally does summon me three days later, I find that we are nearly strangers.

Part VI

Father's Return

Alexandria, in my sixteenth year

Chapter 33

Year 27 of Ptolemy XII

Having Father back in Alexandria after his long exile proves difficult for us all. I am nearly sixteen, a grown woman, and Father has aged greatly. His face is deeply lined and haggard, his hair is streaked with gray, his eyes bloodshot and baggy. That both of us have changed is obvious.

Though they are not fond of Queen Berenike, few Egyptians want to see the man they call Auletes occupy the throne, even though it is rightfully his. Father has always had his loyal supporters as well as the bitter enemies who drove him into exile. The people are still deeply divided in their loyalties, but at this point King Ptolemy XII has the force of an entire army behind him.

I can only imagine his mood as he strides through his palace—the palace that Berenike had done over for herself—and observes the changes made in his absence. He could not have expected an enthusiastic welcome—he is aware that some of his former friends have seized power—but he must be enraged to see that his own daughter has replaced him on the throne. I am very glad not to be in Berenike's position.

Father summons his children to what was once *his* throne room and is now Berenike's, and he lines up the five of us. Tryphaena, of course, is missing, but he does not mention this. The boys stare uneasily at him. Ptolemy XIII and Ptolemy XIV do not recognize Father. He has been away for most of their lives. Arsinoë, at thirteen, is so excited she can hardly contain herself. She giggles and twitters until he turns on her abruptly and growls, "Be quiet, girl! You utter only nonsense!" Her nervous laughter dissolves into tears.

Then his eyes come to rest upon me, and he gazes at me thoughtfully. I bow low and touch his feet, murmuring, "My lord." Father says nothing but merely nods and smiles faintly. I let my breath out slowly, and relief flows through me to the tips of my fingers.

Next, he turns his attention to Berenike. She is as pale as death. When she follows my example and bows, reaching out to touch his feet, her hands are trembling. "Welcome back, dear father," she says. Her voice is trembling too.

"Thank you, Queen Berenike." He utters the word "queen" as though it leaves a bitter taste in his mouth, and waits for her to say more.

Father's black look cuts through her like a dagger. She sees it and understands its meaning. She drops to her knees, weeping, and crouches in front of him. "My lord," she says. She sounds as though she is choking. "I beg you to realize that I meant only to do all I could to take care of our beloved country while you were away, so that when you returned you would find everything just as you would have desired—"

"Silence, liar!" Father roars suddenly, startling everyone. The little Ptolemies jump, Arsinoë gasps, and Berenike falls forward, flat on the floor, babbling incoherently. Father leans down and seizes a handful of her linen tunic and jerks her to her feet. Her eyes are rolling wildly. He releases her, and she staggers, trying to catch her balance. Her teeth are chattering. She is terrified. Now she must face the consequences of seizing power that was not hers to take.

"Explain to me first, please, what has become of your sister Princess Tryphaena?" Father says softly. It would have been less frightening if he had shouted. "I wish to hear from *her* lips what her intentions were on the day that the two of you decided to appoint yourselves corulers in my absence."

Berenike sees a way out of her dilemma. "It was Tryphaena's idea, my king," she says. "I swear to you that I did all I could to dissuade my sister, argued with her that we had no right, no authority! But she was the eldest, the next in line to rule, she had so much more power than I did! But you know how she was, always headstrong, willful, rebellious—"

Suddenly, Berenike turns to me, her eyes wide and pleading. "Would you not agree, Cleopatra? You saw her, did you not? Always demanding more servants, more jewels, more of everything? She was so self-indulgent! And all the time I worked ceaselessly, devoting myself to doing everything possible for our people. It was Tryphaena who hungered for attention and an opulent life, not I! Is that not true, Cleopatra?" she sobs. "Is it not?"

"You describe our sister truthfully," I say, regarding her levelly, this sister who for more than three years has kept me in a constant state of fear for my life. "But now, Berenike, you must describe yourself just as truthfully. Speak to King Ptolemy of your desire for power. Tryphaena wanted luxury and attention, that much is true. But you wanted power, always more of it, and you ridded yourself of her. You had Tryphaena killed—and Titus, too."

King Ptolemy fixes his gaze on Berenike. "You are a traitor and a usurper, Berenike, and for that you must die," he says coldly. He nods to the Roman cavalry officer standing nearby with a half-dozen Syrian soldiers. I had scarcely noticed them until then. "Seize her," the king commands. His voice shows no feeling. It is as though this second daughter is a total stranger to him.

The soldiers instantly surround her. "No! No!" Berenike cries. She screams and struggles as they clamp iron chains onto her wrists. She turns to me, her mouth open in a silent plea, and I see the desperation in her eyes. I pity her. I cannot save her, even if I should wish to, and I do not. I look away as the soldiers drag her off.

Arsinoë anxiously grips my hand. The little Ptolemies stand rigidly, their eyes round with fright. Father dismisses his four remaining children with a wave of his hand. It takes an effort to walk away, especially with Arsinoë clinging to me. The cavalry officer in command of the soldiers steps into my path.

"Marcus Antonius at your service, Princess Cleopatra," he says with a disarming smile.

But I am too distracted to pay the officer any attention. I want to get as far as possible from my father until his anger cools and is replaced by the warmth and tender affection I remember from my childhood. *But will that day ever come?*

Chapter 34

The New Queen

Tension grips Alexandria for days after Father's return and the death of Queen Berenike. Rumors spring up out of nowhere, spread quickly, and disappear just as fast. Irisi and Monifa bring me news from the marketplace, but the rumors change almost daily. It is known throughout the city that Berenike was murdered by order of the king.

Demetrius says the scholars of the Museion are all talking about the Roman officer Marcus Antonius. It was this officer who persuaded King Ptolemy to be compassionate to the defeated people of Pelusium. It was Marcus Antonius who insisted that Archelaus be given a respectful burial after he was killed in battle. But Marcus Antonius bowed to the king's wishes and ordered his lieutenant to end Berenike's life with a dagger through her heart.

Antonius is unable to prevent the murder of many of Father's enemies. "All who opposed me must die," he has decreed. Among them is Antiochus, the grand vizier who served Father for many years. After his death, his property is seized to help pay off the king's enormous debts.

During these turbulent days, I meet Charmion only once, again in the zoological garden near the elephant's cage. I am unsure if some of Berenike's former spies may now be working for someone else.

"We have so much to talk about," I tell Charmion during our brief time together. "I miss seeing you."

"Don't worry, Cleopatra," Charmion says. "There will be time for us to talk later. You have your studies, and I must help the younger dancers."

A month later, the Roman governor of Syria arrives in Alexandria. His name is Gabinius, and he has come to collect the money promised him by King Ptolemy for his help in restoring the king to his throne. Father invites hundreds of people to a banquet in honor of Gabinius, the cavalry commander Marcus Antonius, and a number of visiting Romans. It is the most extravagant banquet since the king's return. Father clearly wants to impress these Romans.

I, too, wish to impress the handsome commander Marcus Antonius. I have had frequent glimpses of him, a few smiles, and even an occasional brief exchange of greetings. Though I have no experience with men, I am strongly attracted to him. I want more.

I dress carefully for the banquet. Father tells me that bare breasts are not the fashion in Rome, and so, though my breasts have become full and I would like to display them as Egyptian women do, I choose not to appear at this banquet in the Egyptian style. Father has brought me a gift from Ephesus, a Grecian gown made of fine silk that hangs in graceful folds. I instruct my hairdresser to arrange my hair as Charmion did, in waves and little curls. Irisi and Monifa go through the jewel chests that once belonged to my two older sisters and select the finest pieces, more beautiful than anything of mine. On each upper arm they clasp a wide cuff made of beaten gold in the shape of a cobra with emeralds for eyes. Around my neck Monifa fastens a collar of gold set with deep blue lapis, and Irisi places the golden circlet of a high-ranking princess on my head.

Because I am fifteen, I am old enough to wear whatever cosmetics I choose, and I like to prepare and apply them myself, as Lady Amandaris taught me. Irisi decorates my feet with henna in pretty patterns, but I decide to leave my hands unadorned, the better to show off the gold and emerald rings that were once Berenike's. The sun has sunk low in the western sky before I am ready. On my way to the banquet hall I stop by a shallow pool and study my reflection in the still water, and I am well pleased with the image of the young woman who smiles back at me. Some may even find me beautiful.

Reassured, I stride confidently toward the banquet hall. All the while, Marcus Antonius is on my mind.

Guards swing open the doors with a flourish. I pause at the entrance. Instead of floor cushions, couches have been provided for the guests to recline on, leaning on the left elbow as they do in Rome. Court musicians begin to play the music reserved for the ranking princess. I am aware that conversation has halted. Heads turn, and every eye is fixed on me. My father rises from his couch as I approach the dais, and at this signal everyone stands. I notice Marcus Antonius near Father's throne, arms folded over his muscular chest, smiling broadly, but I must not allow myself to be distracted. Father holds out his hands to welcome me.

"My daughter Cleopatra, the new queen of Egypt," he announces to his guests.

Not Princess Cleopatra—*Queen!*

I try to conceal my surprise. Father has not spoken to me of this since his return. I thought that perhaps he had changed his mind and decided to take a new wife to rule by his side. He has not had a wife since he sent away the mother of the little Ptolemies. I believed my time would come later. But now the applause of the crowd rings sweetly in my ears, and I acknowledge it with bows. Marcus Antonius seems to me to applaud more vigorously than anyone. I am deeply pleased. This is all just as Father promised years ago: *When I do return, you and I will rule Egypt together.* And when the day inevitably comes that Father is no longer by my side, I am confident that Egypt will thrive under my just and intelligent rule. The people will regard me as they have every pharaoh: half queen, half sacred goddess.

The Romans raise their jewel-studded goblets in toasts to me, to King Ptolemy, to one another. Father spent enough time in Rome to know just what will dazzle his honored guests. The food is varied and plentiful—every dish one can think of, and a great deal of it. It is served on gold plates inset with carnelian and lapis. The excellent wine flows freely. A troupe of dancers enters, wearing nothing but their belts made of shells that jingle as they leap and sway. Charmion leads them. She does not even glance in my direction. But the performance seems to startle the Romans. Is this not the custom in their city?

"One thing I learned during the time I spent in Rome is that the people don't know how to enjoy themselves," Father says to me later in the evening, after the dancers have finished and the feasting has resumed. His words are slurred. "Not the way we do." He rises unsteadily to his feet, produces his *aulos*, and begins to play. Eyes closed, he dances to his own music, a hymn of praise to the god Dionysus.

The Romans, I notice, look even more shocked than before—disgusted, in fact. Toward the end of the night, the only Roman who seems to be thoroughly enjoying himself is the cavalry commander.

Marcus Antonius is an exceptionally fine-looking man—not in the delicate, almost feminine way of Titus or roughly shaggy like Archelaus, but ruggedly masculine. His bold, laughing eyes seem to follow me wherever I go. I cannot resist glancing his way whenever I think he will not notice, but he always does, and rewards me with a mischievous smile. I confess that I like the way he looks at me, admiring my beauty. I delight in his gaze. And I am drawn to him so strongly, I am almost breathless.

Now that Father has returned from exile and taken his rightful place as pharaoh on the throne of Egypt, I feel liberated, free once again to come and go as I please. I plan to revel in this new freedom, not having constantly to look over my shoulder to see if one of Berenike's spies is observing me, possibly about to seize me and murder me. I intend to go out to the royal stables and reclaim Bucephala, now that Arsinoë can no longer threaten me and seems to have lost interest in horses and riding. I will stroll at will through the marketplace, talking to the old woman who sells stew, and visit the harem to spend time with Charmion whenever I wish.

My mind drifts often to Marcus Antonius. I find myself wondering what it might be like to be in his arms, to be kissed by him. I have never before experienced this powerful feeling. *Suppose I invited him to ride out into the desert with me? But how do I go about arranging that?* I will ask Charmion's advice, and her mother's.

But I am mistaken about the freedom I plan to enjoy. I am now the queen of Egypt, expected to fill the role of consort to the king, and I have scarcely any time for myself. My days are full. My encounters with Marcus Antonius are fleeting and never private. Then, just before the commander leaves Alexandria, summoned to Rome by the triumvir Julius Caesar, we happen to meet by chance in the forecourt of the king's palace. I confess that I have been hoping for such a moment. We have just one conversation.

"Queen Cleopatra," says Marcus Antonius, "I have traveled throughout much of the world, and you are the most beautiful woman I have ever seen." He gets down on one knee and takes my hand in both of his. "You will always be the queen of my heart."

He rises, kisses my hand, bows, and leaves without waiting for a response.

"But what did you say to him, Cleopatra?" Charmion asks when I finally have a chance to describe this scene to her.

"Nothing! Not a word!"

Charmion laughs. "The queen of Egypt struck dumb by the words of a Roman soldier? I can't believe that!"

"It's true!" I protest. "What could I have said? That I have fallen in love with him?"

"Have you?"

"I don't know, Charmion. But I have not ever felt this way before."

Charmion has no more words for me. And now the handsome Roman commander is gone. I watched his ship sail out of the harbor and stood gazing at the empty sea long after the ship had disappeared from sight. I doubt that I shall ever see Marcus Antonius again.

Chapter 35

Studies in Ruling

Father has occupied his throne again for more than four months, and I have been at his side for three of them. So far there is little to show for it. Again this year the floods were too low, and as a result the harvest is falling far below normal. The fields are dry, but Egypt is drowning in ruinous debt. Making matters worse, Father has done something of which I strongly disapprove: He appointed Rabirius, the Roman moneylender to whom he owes enormous sums, as the new finance minister of Egypt. I point out the folly of this decision as diplomatically as I can, but Father waves away my suggestion. "You are my consort, not my advisor," he says abruptly.

Everyone despises Rabirius. He dismisses the Egyptians who have done the administrative work of the kingdom for many years, and installs his own men in those positions. He raises taxes again and again. I see the despair on the faces of every man and woman I pass as I make my way through the marketplace. The old woman who sold stew to hungry workers has been reduced to begging. She looks so ragged and sad that I hardly recognize her.

"Young princess!" she calls out to me, forgetting or perhaps ignorant of the fact that I now bear the title of queen. "Please help us!" she pleads.

"I will do my best," I promise her, though there is nothing I can do. It has reached the point that I no longer enjoy strolling among the stalls.

Father sometimes invites me to meetings with his advisors, but my role is simply to listen. Father calls me "queen," yet I have no voice and no power. Privately, though, I have the king's ear. He does not always follow my advice, but he is willing to hear me out.

Father does not want to admit that he has made a serious error, first in borrowing such a vast amount of money, and then by placing the Roman moneylender in charge of Egypt's finances. "Perhaps it would be best to let Rabirius return to Rome, and to bring back our former minister," I suggest in carefully chosen words. "An Egyptian is more likely to place the prosperity of his country above his own."

At last he agrees to my suggestion, and Rabirius departs for Rome. The Syrian governor leaves too, though his soldiers stay on to help quell the unrest that always threatens. Then, even with Egypt's finances near collapse, Father embarks on a massive program of restoring old temples and erecting new ones. The most ambitious building of all is his great marble tomb. I am unable to persuade him to delay at least a year or two.

"I want to be remembered by the people for the good I

have done," he tells me. "And I must be prepared for eternity." He goes almost daily to check on the progress of the tomb and of the funerary boat in which his body will someday be carried. Sometimes I accompany him, at his request, a duty I do not like.

Now he concerns himself with my education—not science and history and the languages that I have been studying for years with Demetrius, but subjects he considers more practical. "You are fifteen. You must learn all there is to know about the country you will someday rule," he says. "Keep in mind that everything belongs to the pharaoh—every grain of wheat and barley that is gathered, every measure of silver and gold dug from the earth, every length of linen woven from the flax in the field." He orders Demetrius to make sure I have a thorough knowledge of the forty-two districts, or nomes, into which Egypt is divided and the names of the nomarchs appointed by the king to administer them. My tutor and I pore over maps of the vast deserts to the east and west of the Nile, showing where gold, silver, copper, precious stones, and minerals lie buried, and I pay attention to how much each mine can be expected to yield. I study scrolls listing the granaries where the grain harvest is stored, the rates at which the farmers are taxed, the methods used to distribute the grain to each town and city.

"Queen Cleopatra will someday make a brilliant ruler," Demetrius boasts to King Ptolemy.

Father is pleased. "I have never doubted it," he says.

Meanwhile, Father has begun trying to bring Arsinoë and me and our two brothers closer together, reminding us that in the eyes of the people we are not ordinary mortals but are semidivine. He gives us new descriptive titles in Greek, meant to emphasize our status and reinforce our power, so that we are worshipped as well as obeyed. This is necessary for me as queen, but I am not yet sure why he gives such titles to my sister and brothers. We are now "New Sibling-Loving Gods." So far there has not been much love among siblings in our family, with two of my sisters dead. We do not speak of them or their deaths. Their names are never mentioned.

When I suggest to Father that he may wish to take a new wife, he merely smiles and shakes his head.

"I have you by my side at the celebration of temple rituals and when we receive visitors from foreign lands," he tells me. "I need no more than that."

Chapter 36

Illness

Two years pass, each day much like the one before it and the one that follows. It is officially Year 30 in the reign of King Ptolemy XII. By the age of seventeen I have settled into my role. Father calls me "my queen" and presents me to rulers from foreign lands who have come to visit our court. I am constantly by his side. Times are still difficult for Egypt—the harvest improved somewhat, though the burden on our people remains heavy. But the hardest thing for me is watching Father's declining health. Every day he seems to grow thinner, paler, and weaker. He has become a shadow of the man he was when he returned from exile.

To continue my education, Demetrius put me in the hands of a teacher-physician who tutored me in the art of healing. The physician taught me to find the little throb in the wrist and on the neck, calling it the voice of the heart. From Monifa

I learned to make certain potions derived from plants believed to treat many ailments. But my skills are not sufficient to help Father.

"Why has he suddenly become so thin?" I ask the royal physician. "His flesh melts from his bones; his speech is slurred even without wine. He seems so weary, and he complains of pain."

But the royal physician resents my presence and my questions, which he deigns to answer only vaguely. Father's condition grows worse, almost by the day. When none of the physician's remedies help, he sends for a priest who uses incantations and magic. The priest instructs Father to spend several days and nights in the Serapeum, the temple honoring the god Serapis, known for his powers of healing. Servants carry Father up the many steps to the golden-roofed temple, and he remains there for the recommended time. This does him neither harm nor good.

The day comes when the royal physician takes me aside and tells me that King Ptolemy does not have much longer to live. It is early in the season of Emergence. The floods arrived fully this year, farmers celebrated with festivals, and we are all hopeful of a good harvest as we receive reports that the newly planted fields along the Nile are beginning to turn green.

One evening at sunset, I leave my father's bedside and go for a walk outside the palace. I am tired. The days have been long for me—not only am I the queen consort of a king too ill to perform even the ordinary duties of ruling, but I still spend hours in studies that will help me to be a good and just ruler and to bring prosperity back to my country. Demetrius, too, is growing old and tired, and I know that someday soon I will be alone, with all the problems of Egypt falling heavily on my shoulders.

My walk takes me along the sea wall below my palace, and I recognize not far ahead of me my dear friend Charmion. I have not had time in many months to sit and talk with her as we used to do, to laugh and gossip and dream. I have seen her whenever the dancers entertain Father's guests, but there is never a chance to exchange words, only an occasional knowing glance. With a rush of feeling I realize how much I have missed her, and I call out to her.

"Charmion!"

She turns at the sound of my voice. I dismiss my bodyguards, Sepa and Hasani, who now accompany me wherever I go, and run to meet her. Together we scramble over the rocks by the sea wall and find a little niche where we are protected from the wind that blows steadily from the sea, but we still have a clear view of the harbor. We talk about all that has happened since we were last together, but I notice that things feel slightly different between us. I realize that more than two seasons have gone by, and at least that long since the time before. She uses formal speech instead of the familiar form I asked her to use with me. But I say nothing about it then, because I am caught up in my worries about Father's failing health and his efforts to keep the people from learning about his sickness.

"It is true," Charmion says. "He does not look well. His skin is yellowish."

Puzzled, I gaze at her for a moment. The king has taken great care not to let anyone see this latest symptom of his ill health.

"Charmion, how do you know that?"

"Because I have seen him," she says.

"But where have you seen him? You haven't danced for him for at least two months. In that time he has scarcely left his palace."

She studies her feet, long and graceful in her sandals. The sandals are of high quality, and I notice that she wears a handsome gold ring set with a deep purple amethyst. The ring looks familiar. I reach out and touch her hand, near the ring. Charmion presses her lips together. I notice that her face is streaked with tears.

"It was a gift of King Ptolemy," she says, avoiding my eyes.

"Because he admires your dancing?"

She shakes her head. "Because he admires Lady Amandaris," she says simply. "He comes to visit my mother at the harem—or did before he became so ill. They are lovers."

This comes as such a surprise that for a moment I am speechless. I supposed that my father has many concubines, but it had not occurred to me that he might also have a mistress, or someone he truly cares about. Little wonder he was so angry at Antiochus! I think of the elegant, dark-skinned woman with kind eyes who is Charmion's mother. "Have they been lovers for long?" I ask, trying to sound merely curious.

Her reply is barely above a whisper. "For more than twenty years—since before I was born." She raises her eyes and looks straight into mine. "My mother is descended from Nubian royalty. King Ptolemy is my father," she says.

"You are my father's daughter?" I stare at her, incredulous.

"I am," she says. "You and I are truly sisters, Cleopatra. But I cannot forget that you are my queen and I am your loyal servant."

She kneels at my feet on the rough stones. I reach out to embrace her, and my heart swells with joy. For this moment at least, I am not alone.

Chapter 37

Death of the King

On the eighteenth anniversary of my birth, the Festival of Isis, I make a special offering to the goddess with whom I identify more and more closely. Months have passed with no improvement in Father's health. I sit at his bedside for long hours as he drifts in and out of wakefulness. He whispers bits of advice, broken phrases, an occasional name. "The Romans," he murmurs. "Pompey was my friend. Trouble between him and Julius Caesar. Caesar, most powerful man in Rome. Perhaps in the world. Your ally or your enemy." Father smiles weakly and squeezes my hand. "Make him your friend."

When the time finally comes for King Ptolemy XII to draw his last breath, I am at his bedside. I am prepared for his death, but when I realize that his *ka*—his life force—has left his body, I am overcome by grief. Nevertheless, I gather my strength and go out to meet the members of his court.

Thoughts of all that lies ahead of me must be set aside as we enact the ancient rituals of death.

Everything has been well prepared. Soon after he returned from exile four years ago, Father ordered the construction of his tomb and the coffin in which his mummified body was to be laid, along with the four alabaster jars to contain his organs, and all the other objects and provisions to be placed with him for his journey through eternity. Now, for days after Father's earthly life has ended, the high priests conduct the prescribed ceremonies with great solemnity. As King Ptolemy waits to enter the afterlife, his heart will be weighed against a feather by the goddess Maat. If his life has been good—and I believe that, in spite of his many faults, my father lived a decent life—then his *akh*, his transfigured spirit, will begin its celestial journey in the company of the Sun God Ra. The king is no longer semidivine; now he is wholly divine. In death the pharaoh has become a god.

Father's carefully prepared body has been placed in two mummy cases, one inside the other, both richly decorated with gold, and carried through the streets of Alexandria in a somber procession. I walk with Arsinöe and our two young brothers behind the king's mummified body while a corps of drummers keeps a slow, steady beat. Not everyone in the crowds lining the Canopic Way looks as though he is mourning the death of a king, but I know at least two faces that are marked by grief: Charmion and Lady Amandaris. Our eyes meet for a moment before both of them bow deeply.

I would give a great deal to have Charmion with me during these long ceremonies, but that is not possible—she is not recognized as the daughter of the king, because the king himself did not formally acknowledge her as his child. Instead, I must endure the presence of my sister and the two boys. Arsinoë, soon to be sixteen, is no longer the sweet, eager-to-please little girl I remember. She has changed a great deal. She does not have the calculated coldness of our older sisters, but she is shrewd and stubborn, and her tutor-guardian, Ganymede, makes the most of it. As I predicted, she is also beautiful. Whenever she happens to be around one of the Syrian officers, she smiles and flutters her eyelashes and tosses her curls, little habits she must have learned from Tryphaena and Berenike.

I glance at our two brothers—Ptolemy XIII, just ten, and Ptolemy XIV, not yet nine—grimly enduring the long ceremony. They are under the guidance of their tutor, Theodotus, who has been with them for most of their lives. I have only slightly more regard for him than I do for Arsinoë's Ganymede. The ambition of these guardians is boundless, and I know that I must be wary of them both.

After Father's body is placed in his tomb and the last rituals are performed, his will is read out. We all know what to expect: I am no longer simply queen consort, but coruler with Ptolemy XIII. Father did not wish me to rule alone, and according to the terms of his will, I must marry my ten-year-old brother, who will be advised by three regents. I intend to delay formalizing the union for as long as possible. Ptolemy XIII will be my husband in name only. By the time he is old enough to take on the roles of husband and king in five years, I shall have everything firmly in hand. I will bring to the throne the ancient traditions of a long line of Egyptian pharaohs stretching back thousands of years and blend those traditions with the brilliance of the Greeks, whose genius was first brought to

Egypt from Macedonia, the land of my ancestors, by Alexander the Great.

I am painfully aware that this glorious heritage has been tarnished in recent generations. Many place most of the blame on my father and the ruinous debt under which he has buried Egypt. But no matter where the fault lies, I will change all that. My deepest desire is to win back the trust and confidence of the people—Egyptians, Greeks, Jews, foreigners—and to restore Egypt to her former magnificence. I intend to be remembered as a great queen.

Year 30 of Ptolemy XII has ended.

Now begins Year 1 of the reign of Cleopatra VII.

Part VII

The New Pharaohs

Upper and Lower Egypt in my eighteenth year

Chapter 38

Coronation

Soon after King Ptolemy XII's death and burial, I show my devotion to my father's memory in the Greek manner by adding the descriptive "Father Loving" to my name. I am now titled Queen Cleopatra VII Philopator. Then, during the festival of the Opening of the Year, between the end of the season of Harvest and the start of the Inundation, Ptolemy XIII and I travel with the royal court to Memphis in Lower Egypt, where pharaohs have traditionally been crowned. This is the first journey I have made on the royal boat in seven years, since my sisters and I traveled up and down the Nile with Father. It is my brother's first time on board—a thrilling time for him, though a sad one for me as I remember all that has happened since then.

Once in Memphis, Ptolemy XIII and I each accept the double crown of Egypt, the flat red cobra crown of Lower Egypt combined with the tall white vulture crown of Upper Egypt. The ceremony begins just before dawn with the appearance of Sirius, the Nile Star, in the eastern sky.

Ptolemy XIII is filled with excitement—he hardly slept the night before the ceremony—but as the hours pass with the shaven-headed priests chanting their monotonous incantations, and the clamorous music of goat-skin drums and brass cymbals and trumpets, he begins to lose interest.

"This crown is too heavy, Cleopatra," he complains. "When does the feast begin? I'm hungry! Are those priests ever going to stop chanting?"

I squint up at the sky: The sun has barely passed the zenith. We have reached the point in the ceremony where my brother and I are each handed the crook and the flail, symbols of kingship and emblems of the god Osiris, and we hold these symbols crossed over our chests. "There is still much that must happen," I whisper. "We must take the sacred oath, and then the nobles and high officials will swear their loyalty. We kneel by the altar, and incense will be burned. Then we'll be carried through the streets on litters. You'll be expected to acknowledge the crowds that have come out to honor us. The feasting will start sometime after that."

This is not what my brother wants to hear. "Why don't you just order the priest to go quickly?" Ptolemy whines.

"That is not possible," I tell him firmly. Then I am inspired to say, "See how the people are all kneeling with their foreheads pressed to the ground? Keep your eye on them. Anyone who looks up is cursed."

This diversion works for a little while, until he sees the ambassador from Carthaginia, or perhaps it is the minister of Babylonia, lift his head and peer around. "Look! I see one,

Cleopatra!" crows the new pharaoh. "He's cursed! Isn't he? Now he will fall dead!"

The high priest frowns in our direction. I shake my head to let him know nothing is wrong, and the seemingly endless ceremony continues. By the time it does finally end, just as the Great Ra touches the western horizon, young King Ptolemy XIII is sound asleep on his golden throne.

But for me this marks the start of my new life. Let the celebration begin!

Chapter 39

BUCHIS

When the coronation festivities in Memphis are finished, my brother and I continue up the Nile in the royal boat to Thebes for a second coronation in Upper Egypt. After a visit lasting half a month, I persuade Ptolemy to return to Alexandria with his regents. He is as eager to leave as I am to have him gone, and he leaps at the bribe I offer: He can stay on the royal boat under the command of Captain Mshai. I will sacrifice the luxury and make do with a smaller, faster, less well-appointed boat. Privately, I instruct Mshai to proceed as slowly as possible. "Allow my brother to stop as often as he likes and to stay as long as he wants. Do not let Theodotus hurry him." Ptolemy thinks I have made him a great concession. But I do not want him to arrive much before I do.

Then I set sail for the small city of Hermonthis, south of Thebes, going ashore often along the way to call on the local priests and announce my determination to finish many of the temples and other buildings begun by my father. Those building projects earned him the loyalty of the priests, and I hope it will do the same for me.

Hermonthis is the home of the sacred bull, Buchis. When Buchis comes to the end of his life, throughout which he has been fed the finest food and cared for by a host of servants, he is mummified and buried with great ceremony. A young bull, which must have a pure white head and a solid black body, is brought forth and installed as the new Buchis.

I remember when I was a child and word reached Alexandria that Buchis had died. When the new bull was to be dedicated, King Ptolemy sent one of his high-ranking noblemen to represent him in the solemn ceremonies. This time I will attend these ceremonies myself.

I receive a fine welcome in Hermonthis, and my speeches, delivered in Egyptian, are greeted with cheers. Shaven-headed priests robed in white linen and wearing papyrus sandals—leather is not permitted—lead out the young bull. This new Buchis is unruly; several strong young men hang on ropes to keep him from charging into the crowd. Wreaths of flowers are draped over his horns, and little girls run along beside him scattering flower petals for him to trample. Older girls keep up a rhythmic tinkling with finger cymbals, and little boys perform handsprings and somersaults over and around the bull while he snorts and stomps and tosses his massive head. Special attendants walk behind Buchis, collecting his droppings, which are considered sacred.

The occasion is a solemn one, for this is a religious rite. The priests are pleased that I have come, and they show their pleasure by greeting me with *thea*—goddess—added to my title: Cleopatra VII Thea Philopator, "The Goddess Who Loves Her Father."

In the eyes of these devout men I am not merely their queen and semidivine pharaoh but also the embodiment of the great goddess Isis, sister-wife of Osiris, mother of Horus. At the end of the Buchis ceremony I make a special offering to Isis with the promise to honor her in every possible way. It is my desire to live up to the priests' high opinion of me, not only in their eyes but in my own. As I stand before them, arms raised, I am exultant. This adulation is what I have lived for, longed for, all my life. My people will not be disappointed.

Because the country is still in mourning for King Ptolemy XII, I have ordered that no sumptuous feasts be held in my honor. "There will be time enough for that in the future," I tell the priests.

But the truth is that I must return to Alexandria as quickly as I can. My brother has half a month's lead, and though he is in a much slower boat, he may have already arrived in the city. I am sure that Ptolemy's three regents are plotting behind my back to seize control. Before he died, Father appointed a regency council to serve for my brother until he is fifteen and of age to rule. In addition to his guardian and tutor, Theodotus, who has traveled with him, the council consists of Achillas, a thin-lipped Roman general, and the eunuch Pothinus, round as a cook pot and cunning as a snake. All three barely disguise their lust for power. Since Ptolemy is only ten, his regents will have five years to exercise control. It is hard to say which of these men I dislike and distrust most, but they have already gained complete control over Ptolemy. I must find a way to break their hold on him and keep the reins of power in my own hands if I am to restore prosperity to Egypt. The welfare of the people rests entirely on me. I trust only myself, and I am ready.

Chapter 40

RULING

Captain Mshai's son, who is only a few years older than I am, commands the boat on which I am returning to Alexandria. He negotiates the dangerous passage near Dendara without incident, and I am sure he remembers as vividly as I do the whirlpools and the havoc they caused on our journey seven years earlier. He is still surprised, and very grateful, that King Ptolemy did not have his father put to death as a result.

"Hurry," I tell him now. "Hurry, hurry."

We are floating with the current, but young Mshai orders the rowers to assist.

When we pass the Nilometer with the markings on the rock, I see that the water level has scarcely risen. The Nile should be in full flood in this first month of Inundation. I understand that the harvest will be poor again. From my visits to the administrators of each nome on the way up the river, I learned that

Egypt faces serious famine. Last year's harvest filled the granaries only halfway.

Once back in Alexandria, I will have to deal immediately with the kingdom's financial situation, the enormous debts our father accumulated over the years, and the burdensome taxes that weigh heavily on everyone, from the highest-ranking nobleman at court to the humblest peasant in the field.

But first I must deal with Ptolemy and his three regents.

"Hurry, hurry," I implore the captain. Though I am young—just half a year past eighteen—I am well trained and fully confident of my ability to rule. I am impatient. But Mshai can do no more to make the boat move any faster.

In a little more than a month I reach Alexandria, take part in the ceremonies welcoming my return, and lose no time in seeking out my brothers and sister. Arsinoë is plainly jealous of me and may soon become a problem. Ptolemy XIV, the youngest of the family, ignores me. I see at once that Ptolemy XIII comprehends none of the crises we face. He likes to strut around, wearing the double crown, which looks rather silly on such a small boy still with the sidelock of youth. The one thing my brother truly cares about is his stable of fine horses. He has been given a two-wheeled Roman chariot, and his greatest pleasure is racing through the streets and marketplaces of Alexandria, scattering donkeys, carts, vendors, and their wares in all directions. Being king is all a game to him. Fortunately, since he is not of age to rule, he stays out of my way. When we are together, he is insolent, which he had not been just months earlier. I have never been close to my brother-king, but I did not expect him to turn against me. I can see that under the influence of his regents he is doing exactly that.

After Father's return from exile until the day of his death, I spent most of my time with him. Now that he has gone on to the afterlife, sailing across the skies in his celestial boat, my days are taken up by meetings with various ministers. I have named an Egyptian, Yuya, as my grand vizier. He is an experienced administrator and probably as trustworthy as anyone I might have selected. I assume that my other advisors are mostly looking out for themselves. At least one of Ptolemy's three regents attends every meeting. Pothinus is the worst, challenging everything I say.

There are only a few people I can still trust. Demetrius, my lifelong tutor, is completely devoted, but he is growing old and can no longer see well. Monifa, who has been like a mother to me, complains of various aches and pains. Irisi serves me faithfully and agrees with everything I say in her efforts to please, but that does not make her a dependable confidante. At times, when I feel utterly alone and discouraged, I realize how much I miss Charmion. I have not had even a few private moments with her since before Father's death. I have allowed myself to become distracted by my responsibilities, and I determine to change that.

"Come quickly, dear sister-friend," I write, and send the note with Yafeu, my loyal messenger. He returns with her reply: "Before the sun sets."

Charmion enters the forecourt, smiling shyly. She looks different—her hair is not in her usual single braid, and her skin glows as rich as honey. She appears more beautiful than ever. "My queen," she says, bowing low, "it is my honor to serve you."

We settle onto cushions in the garden of the palace where I have lived since childhood. "I've ordered changes in the main palace that was Father's—and, for a short time, Tryphaena's and Berenike's," I explain in answer to her question. "When it's finished, I'll make it my official residence. Meanwhile, it's easier to stay where I am."

A serving girl brings us fruit and refreshing drinks, and I send away the attendants with their ostrich-feather fans. I ask Charmion about the health of her mother. "She is well, my queen," she replies, again returning to the formal style of speech.

I interrupt her, taking her hand in mine. "I thought we agreed long ago that we'd talk together informally, as sisters do. Because we truly *are* sisters, dear Charmion."

"That was before you became Queen Cleopatra VII Thea Philopator," she says. "Now pharaoh and sole ruler."

I frown at her. "Then I order you to speak to me as your sister and not as your queen!" I say sternly. She looks startled for a moment before both of us begin to laugh. Soon we are talking together in the intimate way we once did.

"I understand that the king's will requires you to marry your brother," she says. "Has that taken place? I've heard nothing."

"I'm delaying as long as possible," I tell her, grimacing. "At eighteen I'm expected to have a husband as coruler. Ptolemy XIII was Father's solution to the problem, not mine. He thought it important to continue the Ptolemy line of rulers, and a king from outside the family would change that. Ptolemy XIII is still a child—only ten. The most I can hope for from the boy is that he races his chariot and leaves the ruling to me." I lean toward her, confiding, "But I would give a great deal to have a man by my side who could be a real companion. My life is a solitary one, as you no doubt realize."

"A man like that handsome Roman cavalry officer," she suggests with a knowing smile.

I feel a rush of heat to my face. "I think of him often," I confess. Marcus Antonius also visits me in my dreams, but I do not mention that.

"And I'm certain he thinks of you as well," she assures me. "Perhaps one day soon fate will bring him to you again."

We are silent for a moment, and then I spring to my feet and begin pacing. "Charmion, allow me to direct our thoughts away from the Roman officer with the winning smile. I'm asking you to come to live in my palace, not as a servant but as my friend and confidante. I badly need someone who will not simply tell me what I want to hear, and I know you are that person." I remove the handsome gold collar I am wearing—a collar that Father gave me—and bend to place it around her neck. "Accept this as a token of my affection for you and the bond of blood that we share."

But she backs away from me, protesting, "My queen, I cannot accept this gift. I am honored that you wish to have me live near you, but I believe I can be of greatest service to you as a dancer at the royal banquets, with my eyes and ears open. And I will gladly come to you whenever you summon me."

Her refusal amazes me. "I could order you to do this," I remind her, "and you would be forced to obey. But I see you've already gone against my order that you speak to me familiarly, like a sister."

"I'm sorry. I forget," she says. "But my queen—Cleopatra—I believe you just said that you need someone who won't just tell you what you want to hear. I'm truly that person. You cannot now order me to be someone else."

"Dear Charmion, you're right!" I admit, laughing. "Nevertheless, I do order you to take this collar. I believe our father would want you to have it."

I fasten the collar around her neck, and I am about to refill our glasses when Arsinoë bursts upon us, uninvited and unannounced. "What are you two talking about?" she demands rudely.

"How beautiful you have become, Princess Arsinoë," Charmion replies smoothly, and begs our permission to leave. I grant it reluctantly, though I can understand why she would not want to stay.

Arsinoë does not fail to notice the gold collar Charmion is wearing. "You gave her that, didn't you? You give her, a common dancer, more than you give me," she complains. "Her mother is nothing more than a concubine!"

I hold Ganymede responsible for Arsinoë's insolence. But to quiet her I make her a gift of a bracelet that once belonged to Berenike, and she leaves the forecourt with an air of victory.

Chapter 41

CHALLENGES

I had not expected ruling my country to be so difficult. The problems I am confronting have tangled roots that reach back years. Most pressing is another poor harvest. The Inundation again fell far below normal and the grain crops failed, as they often have in recent years. Now farmers cannot pay their taxes, people are hungry, and peasants are leaving their lands and streaming into the city, demanding food. This angers the Alexandrians, who blame me for the shortages and the unrest—as though I have the power to command the waters of the Nile to rise and the crops to flourish!

There is also the problem of my brother, Ptolemy XIII. In the months after Father's death, when I first became queen, it was easy to ignore my ten-year-old brother and to rule alone, as I intended. But now, over a year into my reign, Ptolemy has grown increasingly arrogant, and I blame this on his three regents. Though I mistrusted them all along, I underestimated them. Their treachery becomes evident when, in order to quell the growing turmoil in the city, I issue a decree ordering grain in the nomes to be shipped only to Alexandria. Until now, mine has been the sole signature on official documents. Now I discover that Ptolemy's regents have succeeded in placing his name on the decree, where I should sign.

"How dare you!" I demand when I see what has been done. I toss aside the stylus, refusing to add my signature.

"Because I am king," retorts my brother smugly. "And you are only the queen."

Smirking, Theodotus retrieves the stylus and holds it out to me. I snatch it from him, scrawl my signature on the papyrus, and stalk out of the hall.

That is only the beginning. My brother's popularity among the people seems to be growing. Nothing is turning out as I planned. If only the rains would fall far to the south in the headwaters of the Nile and the floods would return and nourish the land, then the granaries would again burst with grain to feed the people!

But it does not happen, and I do not know what to do. My advisors argue among themselves. Egypt has always fed the world, and now it cannot feed itself.

Adding to my burden, the news reaching us from Rome is deeply disturbing. The crushing debt incurred by my father—ten thousand talents plus the interest, which I have not even bothered to calculate—has not been reduced by so much as a single silver drachma. Moreover, two of the Roman triumvirs are reported to be at each other's throats, Julius Caesar against Pompey. How I wish Father were here to offer counsel!

He knew these men well—Pompey had become his friend, even taking him into his home. Would he have approved my decision to send military aid to Pompey, which has further enraged the Alexandrians?

The months pass, and the people question everything I do. The latest decree on my writing table does not even require my signature. My brother's stands alone.

It is a dangerous time. I am twenty, I have been the ruling queen for two years, and I find I cannot even trust my own advisors. *Who is my friend and who is my enemy? Is my grand vizier, Yuya, plotting behind my back?* I invite members of my court to banquets, as I am expected to do, but I am always on guard for poison in my cup or the sudden thrust of a dagger.

Charmion remains my sole confidante. I often send for her late at night, after I have dismissed my servants and sleep will not come. She prepares a warm infusion of mint and honey that helps me to relax, and she listens, saying little, while I talk.

"The people question everything I do!" I tell her, pacing restlessly. "Pothinus slyly turns them against me. What shall I do? Tell me, dear friend! What do you advise?"

Charmion is silent, her feet curled under her, sipping her warm drink as I continue to pace. "Perhaps you should leave Alexandria," she says quietly.

I stop short and whirl to face her. "What? And let my enemies see that they have defeated me? Never!" I commence pacing again.

"Just temporarily," she replies. "Only for a little while, until people have had a chance to calm themselves. Let them see the trouble Ptolemy will create in your absence. They will come to their senses soon enough."

"And if they don't?" I stare at her. "If you were not my best friend, I would have you seized as a traitor."

"But I *am* your best friend, and I think you should finish your tea and lie down. I will stay here and watch over you while you sleep. We will talk again in the morning."

I obey, too tired to object. "You know, Charmion," I murmur as she draws a silk coverlet over me, "sometimes I wonder if my life would not be easier if I had a true partner to share the burden of ruling. Not my dull-witted brother, who is merely the puppet of his advisors, but a strong, intelligent man."

"Have you anyone in mind for the role?" she asks, smiling.

"No," I confess, though a fleeting image of the handsome Roman officer I met nearly a half-dozen years ago passes through my mind.

And then, grateful for her presence, I sleep.

Chapter 42

Ptolemy's Banquet

It becomes a ritual. I work ceaselessly, meeting with subjects who wait their turn to complain and to plead, listening to my advisors, poring over official documents, struggling to avoid a direct confrontation with my brother's regents. Then, late at night, too tired even to sleep, I send for Charmion.

One night my messenger, Yafeu, runs back from the harem with a message, not from Charmion but from Lady Amandaris: "Charmion has been ordered to dance for the king's banquet."

"The *king's* banquet?" This is a surprise, and not a pleasant one. "I know nothing of this. What is the occasion? Where is it being held? Who is attending? I want the answers, without delay!"

Yafeu hurries off again, and I pace the rooms of my palace, growing angrier and angrier, until at last he returns with a report. "The banquet is in the great hall of the king's palace in celebration of Year 1 of the reign of King Ptolemy XIII. The three regents sit by the king's side on the dais. The highest nobility are present." Yafeu hesitates.

"Yes? Is there more?"

"It is my duty to tell you, my queen, that the banquet has been going on for some time. The guests are . . . somewhat overindulged in wine."

I am so furious I can scarcely speak. *Year 1 of the king's reign! Outrageous!* It is, in fact, Year 2 of *my* rule. "By whose order is it no longer the rule of Queen Cleopatra VII Thea Philopator?"

Poor Yafeu backs away from my rage. "I do not know, my queen." He waits stoically for my next order. Mustering my self-control, I dismiss him with thanks. Then I awaken Irisi and Monifa to help me dress. Still half-asleep, the women protest feebly that my gowns have not been hung up and prepared, that the hairdresser is not available, that no one is around who can apply my cosmetics.

"I shall do it myself," I snap. I snatch up the first gown I lay my hands on and begin to put it on.

Irisi comes to assist me. "What is happening, mistress?" she asks sleepily.

"My brother is entertaining at a banquet celebrating his reign. He has neither invited me nor notified me of this insult."

Usually, I take great care applying cosmetics, but on this night I dash a smear of malachite on my eyelids, hastily outline my eyes with a thick line of kohl, and set the gold circlet with the upright cobra, symbol of my queenship, on my brow. I remember my royal ring, but in my rush I forget my sandals.

Hurrying barefoot across the open courtyard toward the great hall, I see Charmion running toward me, her long braid flying. "Please do not go there, my queen, I beg you," she says, making a quick bow. "It may be a trap."

I am much too incensed to take her advice. "Wait for me in my quarters," I tell her. "I'll talk with you later." And I hurry on.

Some of the royal musicians are resting by the entrance to the hall. They glance up—startled, I suppose, to see me—but they remember to bow low.

"Play something," I shout at them.

"But King Ptolemy has dismissed us," one of the horn players says.

"And I, Queen Cleopatra, order you to play! Where are the cymbals? The drums? Come, come, musicians, announce the arrival of your queen!"

The trumpeters obediently sound the notes signaling the arrival of the sovereign, and I sweep into the great hall. The hall is crowded, as it was when Father held banquets here, and I recognize almost everyone present: courtiers, noblemen, the wealthy and influential of Alexandria, those who fawned over Father when he was alive and spoke ill of him as long as he was in exile. Ptolemy's three regents, Theodotus, Achillas, and Pothinus, are lounging on their elbows in the manner of the Romans and gaze at me with bemused expressions. My brother is drunk, barely able to sit upright on his throne. *Who decided to give the boy too much wine?*

I expect them all to rise and bow, but no one stirs. Finally, fat Pothinus pushes himself to his feet and waddles toward me. "Welcome to King Ptolemy's banquet, Queen Cleopatra," he lisps. He pronounces my title with heavy sarcasm and wiggles his ringed fingers. "We were just about to send for you, were we not, my king?"

Ptolemy rouses briefly, his eyes unfocused, and mumbles something unintelligible. His head droops down on his chest again.

"Then I am happy to have arrived at precisely the right moment, Pothinus. Please continue with your celebration. But first, perhaps you should tell me just what it is you are celebrating without me."

This time Ptolemy wakes up. "I'm king now, Cleopatra," he says. His words are slurred, but I understand him perfectly. "The power's all mine now, not yours." He waves toward his three regents. "Just ask them."

General Achillas answers before I can demand an explanation. "The tide has turned against you, Cleopatra." Not *Queen Cleopatra*; just *Cleopatra*. I suck in my breath when I hear the change in his tone. "The Alexandrians no longer believe in you. You would be well advised to gather up your supporters—if you still have any—and leave this city."

I glance toward Theodotus, whom I have known since my own childhood. He will not look at me. "Yes," he says, his eyes averted. "Go, Cleopatra."

I turn my back on Ptolemy and the three regents and stride out of the hall as regally as one can when barefoot. I have come to fear my brother, deeply influenced as he is by the three men who obviously have neither love nor loyalty for me. Too young to realize what he is doing, Ptolemy has been manipulated into declaring himself the sole ruler. But the Alexandrians are supporting him, and this wounds me. Alexandria, my birthplace, my city, my heart! I understand that Charmion is right: I have no choice but to leave it—for now.

PART VIII

THE QUEEN'S FLIGHT

Ashkelon, the land of the Philistines,
at the start of my twenty-first year

Chapter 43

At Sea

There is no sleep for me that night, after Ptolemy's banquet. Irisi and Monifa, now wide awake, take charge of the packing. My bodyguards, Sepa and Hasani, have been alerted, as have cooks, stewards, and other servants. I send Yafeu to contact the few people I am absolutely certain are loyal to me. Captain Mshai has been ordered to round up a crew, saying that the queen is planning a leisurely journey up the Nile. To mislead Ptolemy XIII and his three regents, should they decide to pursue me, we plant rumors that I am leaving Alexandria and am on my way to Thebes. But Thebes is not my destination. I intend to leave Egypt.

Within three days everything is ready for my departure. I do wonder if anyone will try to stop me, tie me up, and throw me into prison—or worse.

Charmion insists on going too, though I have warned her

it could well be a dangerous journey. I am glad she will be with me. "You seem very calm, mistress," she remarks when she returns from bidding Lady Amandaris good-bye. We climb into our chairs to be carried to the royal boat. The stars are beginning to fade in the pink-tinted dawn sky.

"Do I?" I ask with a smile. "I've never been more afraid, Charmion. But this is not the time to yield to fear. It's the time to *act*."

Our bearers, alert for threatening figures in the shadows, make their way to Lake Mareotis. I board the gilded boat without any of the ceremony that usually accompanies the comings and goings of royalty. The captain guides the boat through the web of canals connecting the spreading branches of the mouth of the Nile, until we reach a protected inlet near the Mediterranean at a point halfway between Alexandria and Pelusium. Those two harbors are well guarded, and it would be impossible to sail out of either city undetected.

In the marshy delta we leave the royal boat. It is large and luxurious, but it is designed for river travel and is not suitable for navigating rough seas and ocean storms. Young Mshai, the captain's son, had gone on ahead and prepared a seagoing galley for us. While the elder Mshai takes the royal boat toward Thebes, without passengers and with only a skeleton crew, to deceive my brother and his regents, my friends and I board the smaller but more rugged ship. Our voyage continues eastward, following the coast, by sail when the winds are favorable and by oar when they are not. We are heading toward the land of the Philistines.

I have never been at sea. If I were not so worried about what lies ahead, I might enjoy the steady pitch and roll as the ship plows through the choppy waters. But I have too much on my mind to take pleasure in this new experience. On one of these restless nights at sea, I note that I am now twenty-one years old, and I contemplate—as I always do on the anniversary of my birth—what the coming year may hold for me and for Egypt.

Chapter 44

Ashkelon

After several days of rough seas with the sturdy galley pitching and rolling sickeningly, we arrive in the port of Ashkelon at the eastern end of the Mediterranean. The anchor is let down, and I am rowed ashore to be welcomed by the governor of this Philistine city-state and by whatever other officials have gathered to witness the unexpected arrival of a queen. I plan to establish my headquarters here while I prepare my next move, though I have only the vaguest idea of what that will be. Charmion and I settle into the simple lodgings offered by the governor, probably the best he has available. But I am not concerned by the lack of luxury. At last I feel safe. No one will harm me here.

Monifa and Irisi wander through the marketplace, alert for rumors, while my bodyguards pass their time by the docks, where traders exchange news as well as goods. For a time we learn nothing of interest. In fact, several months pass with little news and nothing to occupy me. I am restless. I wonder about the mood in Egypt and worry about what my brother-king is doing. It is now the season of Inundation in Egypt, hot and humid in Alexandria but even hotter in Ashkelon. I move into a tent near the beach, hoping for the cool sea breezes I enjoyed in my palace. There are none. Every day, I grow more impatient, more irritable. This is surely not what my father intended.

"I should be back in Alexandria," I fret to Charmion. "The people need me."

"You must be patient, Cleopatra. You will know when the time is right," she assures me, and I try to accept her wisdom. But the restlessness stays with me. I cannot imagine how my father endured years of exile.

Then, one day, my bodyguards rush back from the waterfront with the report that two armies led by generals of the Roman triumvirate, Pompey and Julius Caesar, have met and clashed in Greece.

"Pompey had twice as many men as Caesar," Hasani tells me. "The bloody battle raged through a long day. But Caesar proved to be the better general and easily defeated Pompey."

"So it is over, then. Caesar is the victor." I cannot see that this has anything to do with me or with Egypt. I reach for a bunch of grapes and pluck them off one by one.

"Not entirely finished, my queen. Pompey is on his way to Egypt to visit your brother. They say he expects a hero's welcome from the son of his old friend Ptolemy XII."

"In Alexandria?" I ask, suddenly alert.

"No, my queen. Pompey's ship is already well to the east of Alexandria. Ptolemy and his army are marching toward Pelusium, where they expect to meet your army and defeat you.

Or so everyone says. And that is where Pompey hopes to meet young Ptolemy."

My army? My thirteen-year-old brother wants to go to war against me? The news stuns me. Ptolemy must be mad! "Hasani, as you well know, I do not have an army!"

My guard smiles. "I have every confidence that Queen Cleopatra will soon raise one."

It is not easy to raise an army under such circumstances, but the alternative is to give in to my enemies and allow my brother to rule in my place. I return the guard's smile, my mind already racing. "You are right, Hasani. I will do exactly that."

Now I know what my next move will be.

I set to work immediately. I have learned that I can be remarkably persuasive when I must.

I arrange a banquet, to which I invite the high officials of Ashkelon and neighboring Philistine towns and villages. My cooks begin preparing a feast. Charmion finds talented young girls in the city and teaches them some simple dances; the musicians who travel with my small court are capable of producing fine music with few instruments. On the night of the banquet the guests gather in a large tent I have had set up and well furnished. When everything is ready, the musicians signal my entrance. I appear among my guests dressed simply but elegantly, wearing little jewelry but the gold crown with the cobra symbol. Still, I sense that my guests are suspicious of me and wonder what I want of them.

After the officials have enjoyed plenty of food and drink and an evening of entertainment and appear content and at their ease, I rise and address them in their language. This makes an excellent impression. They listen intently.

"I have been driven out of my country by usurpers who have chosen to ignore the provisions of the will of my father, King Ptolemy XII," I tell them. I continue speaking in this manner, as I see they are being swayed in my favor. Even before I have finished, my guests have pledged hundreds of soldiers—mercenaries who, for payment, will fight in my name.

In the following days, while my newly recruited troops are being provisioned, runners bring frequent reports from Pelusium. Achillas, one of my brother's regents, is waiting there at the head of Ptolemy's army. The other two regents, Pothinus and Theodotus, are also with him. They expect my army to march westward, toward Pelusium, and they are preparing for the battle.

Then, one morning, several members of my advance guard arrive, dragging with them one of Ptolemy's soldiers. He is in terrible condition, begging for food and water. They bring him to me, asking what should be done with him.

"Give him what he wants," I order. "But only after he tells me what my brother and the regents plan to do now."

The guards fling the miserable soldier at my feet. Finding himself in the presence of his queen, he struggles to give me the information I want: After being defeated by Julius Caesar, General Pompey arrived in Pelusium, asking to see the son of his old friend.

"And did my brother agree to see him?"

The poor fellow shakes his head. "Pothinus would not allow it. He feared that Pompey was more likely to support *you*, my queen." He halts, gasping, and I motion the guards to give him a sip of water. "And so an evil thing was done." The informant stops again and bows his head. He appears to be near collapse.

"Do go on!" I cry. "Tell me what happened!"

"Pothinus invited Pompey to come ashore. When he did, Pothinus ordered his men to run the Roman general through with a sword, cut off his head, and throw his body into the sea."

"They murdered Pompey in this manner?" The horrible story makes me ill.

The soldier nods. "They did, my queen."

"And King Ptolemy? What did my brother do?"

"Nothing, my queen."

"Nothing?" My voice rises, trembling with anger. I take a deep breath and struggle for control, knowing that I must be strong. Weakness is a luxury I cannot allow myself. "Where is Pothinus now?"

"Pothinus and Theodotus are on their way to Alexandria with the preserved head of Pompey. Pothinus wants to present it to Caesar as a trophy. They hope to win his favor."

These men have preserved Pompey's head for Caesar? *To win his favor? Do these terrible men have no sense of honor or righteousness? Have they gone mad?* I glare at the miserable informant and order him taken away.

"One day, Pothinus and Theodotus will have to deal with me," I say. My voice is hard and cold, despite my fury. So, too, will King Ptolemy, I think. And Caesar, as well.

But first I must return to Alexandria. As Charmion promised, I know the time is right. The question is how to get there safely.

Chapter 45

Caesar's Orders

Six Roman soldiers, stumbling with fatigue, present themselves at the entrance to my tent. Their captain, explaining that they have been sent by Julius Caesar, delivers a letter. Warily, I break the seal. Caesar writes in Latin, summoning me to Alexandria in language that makes clear my refusal is not a choice.

I sit down and write a brief reply, also in Latin, "I do as Caesar commands," sign it Queen Cleopatra VII Thea Philopator, and hand it to the officer. "And my brother, King Ptolemy XIII?" I ask. "Has Caesar summoned him as well?"

"My orders are only to deliver the letter," the captain answers stiffly. "I have no knowledge of the contents, and I have no other information."

When the Roman soldiers leave, I send Monifa with instructions to have them fed well before they begin their journey back to Caesar, wherever he is. I ask Charmion to organize a little musical entertainment for them and to let me know when sleep begins to overtake them.

Late in the evening, she comes to tell me the soldiers are yawning, one or two already snoring. Dressed in a simple gown, I find my way alone to their captain's quarters. He leaps to his feet, startled to see me.

"I beg your pardon for disturbing you, Captain," I say. "I have come to wish you a good night's rest and a safe journey back to Alexandria. I, too, will be making that journey quite soon, on the orders of Julius Caesar." I smile winningly. "May I sit down?"

He gapes at me in my revealing gown and swallows hard. "You are most welcome here, Queen Cleopatra," he manages to say.

I settle comfortably in the officer's chair and take time to gaze around the small field tent. "I wonder if you might have a little wine left from the evening meal. If not, I shall send for more." In fact, before visiting the captain's tent, I had sent him another jar of wine, the last from the supply I brought with me from Egypt. The captain eagerly fills two goblets on his table, and I raise mine in a toast. "To noble Caesar."

"To noble Caesar!" echoes the captain.

I take a tiny sip of wine. "It will be a great privilege to meet him at last. My father, King Ptolemy XII, always told me that Julius Caesar is the greatest general since my own ancestor, Alexander."

"What you say is true," replies my guest. "It was my honor to serve under Caesar during his conquest of the Gallic tribes. There is no more brilliant general alive today. Certainly he has just proved that he is more skillful than Pompey, whose forces outnumbered Caesar's two to one."

"I do not wish to talk about the unfortunate Pompey," I tell him. "Nor do I wish to discuss the despicable man responsible for his murder. I am hoping, my good captain, that you can advise me which way to proceed, since you have come most recently from Pelusium."

The captain drinks deeply. "You are a wise queen," he says, leaning toward me, "as well as a beautiful one." I pretend to be flattered and let him continue. "King Ptolemy has already returned to Alexandria, traveling with the man you so much despise, Pothinus. Ptolemy's army remains behind in Pelusium under the command of General Achillas. The general expects you to attack with the mercenaries you have recruited here."

"And Caesar? Has he arrived in Alexandria?"

Soon I have extracted the whole story, or at least the parts of it known to my friend the captain. He tells me that Julius Caesar was welcomed to my city by that dog-eating Pothinus, who made a great show of offering him Pompey's head. "Caesar turned his eyes away from the head and shed many tears over his fallen adversary," the captain reveals. Then, he continues, "Caesar has taken over the royal palace. It is to the royal palace that he has summoned you and Ptolemy XIII to appear."

"For what reason? Can you tell me that, Captain?"

The captain has had too much to drink and his tongue is loosened. He may not know the reason officially, but he certainly has some ideas on the subject.

"Caesar desires that you and Ptolemy XIII rule together as husband and wife."

None of this is good news, but at least I now have some sense of where the players are in this complicated game. "What do you suggest I do, Captain, in order to reach mighty Caesar?"

The captain spreads a map on his knees. "Gather your army and proceed to the south of Pelusium," he says, "thereby avoiding Achillas and his men." I nod encouragingly, and the officer sketches a route for me.

I thank him warmly and promise to follow his advice. Then, pleading weariness, I leave the captain with wishes for a refreshing night's sleep.

Charmion is waiting for me in my tent. I repeat my conversation with the Roman officer. "Will you follow the captain's advice, my queen?" she asks.

"Of course not."

"You don't trust the captain?"

"It's not that I don't trust him . . . It's true, I don't! I simply have a better plan. We will travel back to Alexandria by sea, but not in our galley. We will go in a fishing boat, disguised as fishermen."

Part IX

The Queen's Return

Alexandria, at the end of my twenty-first year

Chapter 46

DISGUISES

Nearly eleven months after fleeing from Alexandria, I prepare to return to Egypt, ready to take up any challenge that Julius Caesar or my brother may hand me.

Sepa and Hasani go down to the beach to hire a fishing vessel barely large enough to carry me and a small group of servants back to Alexandria. Monifa and Irisi visit the market and bargain for fishermen's clothing. They pack up the little we are able to carry with us and arrange to have the rest put aboard the galley in which we arrived in Ashkelon. Young Mshai, along with my hairdresser, musicians, and others, are to wait fifteen days before leaving Ashkelon for Alexandria.

I confer with the most experienced Philistine officer and instruct him to march with the hired soldiers to Pelusium and engage Ptolemy's army. "Keep Achillas occupied," I tell him. "Defeat him if you can, or distract him if you cannot."

The fishing boat is crowded, dirty, and smelly in spite of Monifa's earnest efforts to make it comfortable. The journey is wet and miserable. For days I am too seasick to care. Slowly, we make our way westward along the coast, stopping at night in small coves and tiny villages. The cook prepares fresh-caught fish and whatever else can be found. Any Roman or Egyptian vessels that might be looking for me pay no attention to this crude boat; they would have learned that I sailed eastward in a galley and would no doubt be watching for it.

I worry about what lies ahead for me. Irisi chatters incessantly, but Charmion is very quiet. I believe they, too, are afraid, though we do not speak of our fears, lest they master us.

After many wretched days at the mercy of wind and waves, we see the first faraway beams of light from the Pharos lighthouse piercing the black night. My impatience almost overcomes me, but I force myself to be calm. After two more stormy days, the beacon guides us to the entrance to the Great Harbor of Alexandria. Sepa and Hasani try to persuade me to wait in the fishing boat outside the mouth of the harbor while they row to shore and report back on what they find.

"I will go with you," I inform them.

My bodyguards are determined that I must stay where I am. "Look, my queen—do you see those boats patrolling the shore? It is much too dangerous."

But I need to see for myself what sort of situation is waiting for me. Eventually I will have to go ashore, and I am convinced that I must do it now rather than later. "No one is expecting me to appear like this."

"I'll come as well," Charmion says firmly. "You should not go about as a lone woman."

I do not argue but move aside to make room for her in the tiny boat.

The sky glitters with stars, but only a thin sliver of moon hangs over us. We battle our way past the rough waves at the entrance to the Great Harbor and glide quietly through the black water, passing near a fleet of warships that I do not recognize. Wet and shivering, we clamber ashore over the rocks. For the rest of the night we try to stay hidden, waiting until the sky bleaches to pale silver and the first rays of the sun appear above the horizon. As the city awakens and people begin to move about, Charmion and I change into Irisi's rough linen clothes, and with my bodyguards still dressed as fishermen—and smelling like them too—we walk into the marketplace. It has been a long time since I have done this, but I find it easy to move about unrecognized. I am in my city again, and that calms me and gives me courage.

Sepa and Hasani buy bread and beer from a vendor and inquire casually about the warships blocking the entrance to the harbor. "Pothinus ordered the ships," my bodyguards report. "He is expecting to seize Queen Cleopatra when she arrives in her galley. You have slipped right under his nose."

This would be amusing if it were not so frightening.

But even in disguise it will not be easy to continue avoiding detection during the long daylight hours. I plan to wait until dark and then find a way to meet with Caesar without my brother's knowledge. I am determined to persuade Caesar that I, Cleopatra VII Thea Philopator, am the true and rightful ruler of Egypt. But what am I to do until nightfall?

Charmion has the solution. "We will go at once to the harem. You can stay safely in my mother's house during the day, even sleep a little, while we work out a way to arrange a meeting with Caesar."

I agree readily. We leave my bodyguards to bring the rest of my servants safely ashore and to hide them in the Jewish quarter, where they are unlikely to be found. We plan to meet Sepa and Hasani again that night near the lighthouse.

No one gives a second glance to two young women in servants' tunics hurrying toward the harem, and we arrive without incident. Lady Amandaris greets me warmly, and when I see the deep affection mother and daughter show each other, I am frankly envious. I have not known a mother's love since I have been old enough to remember.

Lady Amandaris welcomes us, obviously relieved to see that we are safe, and after we have explained our mission, she arranges for us to bathe. It has been more than a month since I last enjoyed the luxury of soaking in a warm bath. What bliss! When we have put on clean clothes, she brings us food and drink and, as we rest, she adds distressing details to what we already know of the situation in Alexandria.

"Julius Caesar entered the city dressed in a purple cloak trimmed in gold," she says. "His bodyguards marched boldly through the streets, each carrying a bundle of birch rods bound together with an ax—a symbol of his authority, we were told. The people were furious when they found out! Riots broke out all over the city, and several people were killed. But the Romans prevailed—there are four thousand soldiers, and you no doubt saw the fleet of warships waiting in the harbor—and now Caesar has taken over the royal palace. King Ptolemy XIII and the wicked Pothinus have also settled in the royal quarter. I beg you to imagine this—a Roman general living in the house of pharaohs!"

"Father always said that Caesar was an ambitious man." I reach out and take her hand.

"It appears that the king was right," Lady Amandaris agrees.

My strength restored, I am ready now to act. "Why has the great Julius Caesar gone to all this trouble? What does he want here? I believe I can reason with him and convince him that the throne of Egypt is rightfully mine, but I must first meet with him alone and in secret, not before the eyes of the whole world. The two of you must help me devise a plan," I tell them. "I need to find a way to get past the palace guards and into Caesar's private quarters. I want to take him by surprise, when he is unguarded and vulnerable."

Lady Amandaris takes up the challenge. "I understand, and I think I can help you," she says. "You need first to charm Caesar, then to reason with him."

Lady Amandaris surely knows how to charm men! Did she not charm my father for twenty years? How much he must have loved this beautiful lady! "Tell me your idea."

"It is a simple one," she says. "I have an acquaintance, a merchant by the name of Apollodorus, who deals in linen cloth of the finest weave. He told me just a day or two ago that Caesar has ordered new bedding more suitable to the tastes of a Roman general, though I have no idea what that might be. I will propose to Apollodorus that he make an appointment to deliver the linens in person to Caesar tonight. You will be rolled up inside these linens, and in that way he will carry you concealed into the palace and directly to Caesar's quarters. When Apollodorus lays down his burden, he will unroll the cloth in front of Caesar's eyes. And you, my lovely queen, will tumble out. What happens after that is up to you." Lady Amandaris sits back and waits for my reply.

"What you are suggesting is outrageous!" I exclaim, but I cannot help laughing. The more I think about it, the better I like her idea, and before the afternoon is over, I embrace the scheme wholeheartedly. We proceed with the plan.

That same evening the linen merchant arrives at the harem carrying a large bundle. Lady Amandaris has procured for me a white linen sheath made of the sheerest fabric that clings to every curve of my body. We agree that I should not make overuse of cosmetics, except for my eyes. I have no jewels—they are still on the galley with Mshai, now on his way from Ashkelon. But will Caesar believe I am who I claim to be if I have not even the golden circlet with the uraeus to prove it?

Once again, Lady Amandaris offers a solution. "Take this ring," she says, removing the ring from her finger. It is heavy gold, carved with King Ptolemy XII's *shenu*, the symbols for his name. "Your father gave this to me as a token of his affection," she explains. "It will make clear to Caesar that you are truly the daughter of the king."

I embrace this generous-spirited woman and prepare to meet the great general, Julius Caesar, who, I have come to understand, is the most famous man in the world.

Chapter 47

Meeting Caesar

"I can't breathe," I complain from deep inside several folds of linen. "I feel like a mummified body wrapped for burial."

Our plan has been set in motion.

Apollodorus, the linen merchant, leaves his young assistant waiting outside while the package is being prepared for presentation to Caesar. Charmion wants to accompany the merchant and his "parcel," but Lady Armandaris insists that she must remain behind. "Your presence would alert the guards and give away the secret," she says. Instead, Charmion will meet Sepa and Hasani at the lighthouse, as we agreed, describe the plan, and instruct them to wait near the palace, in case I need them.

Once the lengths of cloth have been loosened enough that I will not suffocate and the ends of the roll bound just tightly enough that I am completely hidden, the assistant is summoned and the two men pick up their bundle and begin the walk from the harem to the king's palace. The assistant says nothing about the additional weight of the bundle, though surely he notices.

Guards have been set up all around the palace, and I can hear their muffled voices as the merchant and his assistant make their way through the crowd. I wish I could see where we are and what is happening, but I must trust that this merchant will not decide to turn me over to the soldiers for a price. It has not been explained to me how Lady Amandaris knows this man. I have come to expect treasonous plots, and I experience a moment of panic, nearly shouting for Apollodorus to set me down here and let me take my chances.

But then I hear the great wooden doors of the king's palace creak open on their iron hinges, the slap of leather sandals on the stone floor, exchanges in Latin between Apollodorus and members of Caesar's special guard. Apollodorus does his best to persuade the guard that Caesar has ordered the linens to be delivered at once, this very evening. The guard is skeptical, unconvinced.

I strain to hear the murmured reply when a commanding voice calls out, "Enter!"

That, I think, must be Caesar. Now that the plan is in motion, my nervousness has disappeared, and I feel calm and confident.

We are moving forward again, and the bundle, with me wrapped inside it, is lowered carefully to the floor. The assistant is dismissed. Apollodorus takes his time unrolling the linens, explaining as he does so the fine quality of the flax, the excellence of the weave. With a final flourish, the bundle is opened and I tumble out.

Sprawled on the cool marble floor, I gaze up at the startled man peering down at me with raised eyebrows. Not a young man—perhaps fifty or more—and not handsome, certainly, with thinning hair and a weathered face, but tall and well proportioned, strong featured, and possessing great elegance. And those eyes! They are filled with intelligence and humor.

So this is Caesar!

"Well now, what is this?" he asks.

"Hail, noble Caesar!" I greet him in Latin, rising gracefully, as dancers are taught to do. My gown has slipped off one shoulder, and I hurriedly straighten it. My hair has come unbound and falls loose on my shoulders. "I am Queen Cleopatra VII," I tell him with my most engaging smile. "Welcome to my kingdom."

This is my introduction to Julius Caesar, and his to me. Caesar recovers his composure quickly—he never really lost it—and sends Apollodorus away with thanks and, I imagine, a more than generous payment. He calls for refreshments and dismisses his servants and guards. I wonder briefly if he has at least one guard concealed nearby. But I think not. Caesar is not afraid of me. I doubt that he is afraid of anyone.

I know Caesar's reputation. My father spoke of his brilliant oratory and the skill with which he controlled the Roman senate. King Ptolemy did not like Caesar, but he could not help admiring him. "He succeeds in everything he undertakes," Father once told me.

We begin to talk. We have a great deal to talk about. We discuss the crop failures and the famine that plagues Egypt but not of the military aid I once pledged to his fallen enemy, Pompey. And neither of us mentions my brother.

Somewhere in Alexandria's royal quarter, Ptolemy XIII no doubt sleeps peacefully, believing that I am safely out of the way and that he alone will rule Egypt. Because of him, I need Caesar's support to assure my place on the throne of Egypt. I hope that Caesar also needs me.

Neither of us touches the food in front of us, and we have little interest in the wine. I am here to charm Caesar and to persuade him. It is not my plan to seduce him. Though I am twenty-one, an age at which most women, even queens, have married and borne children, I am inexperienced in the art of love, and Caesar is a man who enjoys a well-deserved reputation for romantic conquests.

As the night goes on, the magnetism between us grows as strong as the pull of the moon on the tides. By the next morning I am Caesar's mistress.

I am not Caesar's conquest. He is mine.

Chapter 48

Brother-Husband

The morning after my first meeting with Caesar, Ptolemy XIII awakens to discover that he has been fooled. When he realizes that I have eluded Achillas's blockade at Pelusium, slipped past Pothinus's warships in the Great Harbor of Alexandria, and somehow arrived in Caesar's bed, my brother unleashes a tantrum. He dashes out into the forecourt of his palace in a rage, flinging his golden diadem to the ground and kicking it aside. This incites an angry outcry from the crowd milling outside the palace gates. I did not foresee this, and I wonder aloud if I should arrange to be smuggled out of the palace in much the same way as I was smuggled in.

But Caesar is unperturbed by the uproar. "I will handle it, Cleopatra," he says calmly. "You are the queen, and you shall remain the queen. Your brother will not displace you. But you must marry him and rule together. It is your father's will and my wish."

This is surely not *my* wish, but I realize that Caesar is right. It is what Father intended.

He steps out onto a balcony and addresses the crowd, demanding order and respect. Once he has quieted the shouting mob and assured them that he will act in their best interests, he orders the guards to disperse them and returns to the bed we shared the previous night.

He gazes down at me. "I want you here with me, Cleopatra," he tells me. He buries his fingers in my hair and breathes in the perfumed scent.

From this time on, events unfold swiftly. The suite of rooms adjoining Caesar's in the king's palace will now be mine. My brother and Pothinus have ordered all my possessions—gowns, robes, cosmetics, jewels, everything—to be tossed into an empty storage granary. I send for Irisi and Monifa, who spent the night in the harem with Charmion, and instruct them to get whatever help they need to move my belongings into my new quarters. If my servants are surprised by this sudden change in my living arrangements, they say nothing but begin to set things right.

I wonder what Charmion is thinking. She surely did not expect this turn of events. But I will wager Lady Amandaris is not at all surprised.

Late that afternoon Caesar summons the ranking noblemen and high officials of Alexandria to gather in the throne room. On Caesar's orders I am seated at his right hand, Ptolemy XIII at his left. My brother, red faced and so angry he can scarcely contain himself, writhes in his chair and refuses to look at me. Two of his regents, Pothinus and Theodotus, are present as well. Achillas is still in Pelusium, fending off my hired troops.

Arsinoë and our younger brother, Ptolemy XIV, sit off to the side, staring at us wide-eyed. Grand Vizier Yuya's bland face registers nothing of what he is thinking.

Magnificent in his gold-trimmed robe of rich purple, Caesar rises and announces that he is about to read aloud the will of King Ptolemy XII. "I am well acquainted with the terms of the will," he says, his voice deep and resonant, "as I was with its author. It is my intent, as well as my solemn duty, to see that the terms of the will drawn up by your late king are carried out."

Caesar reads out the document, which is quite brief. This is the second time the will has been read publicly since Father's death three years earlier. My brother was ten years old then, and I intended to delay formalizing any marriage for as long as I could. But it may no longer be possible. There can be no arguing with my father's wishes or with Caesar's decision: *Ptolemy XIII and Cleopatra VII are to rule together as husband and wife and as equals.* This does not please Ptolemy any more than it pleases me. He throws me a look of pure hatred. But Ptolemy is still just thirteen, and were he not controlled by his scheming regents, I would not consider the unhappy arrangement anything but a minor problem.

Caesar has something more to say: Arsinoë and eleven-year-old Ptolemy XIV are to become king and queen of Cyprus. They look at each other, stunned. Though I had not expected this, I welcome it. I no longer trust Arsinoë any more than I did Tryphaena or Berenike, and I will feel much safer with my troublesome younger sister sent away to rule a distant kingdom.

A month after Caesar makes this announcement, a public celebration accompanies my marriage to my brother. The ceremony involves only placing our signatures on a papyrus scroll, but the common people of Alexandria expect wine to flow in the streets, animals to be slaughtered and roasted in open pits, and street musicians to provide entertainment, and so I order it.

Before the so-called celebration begins, Charmion comes to me, the first I have seen her since Lady Amandaris arranged my delivery to Caesar's quarters. She bows low and then kneels. "I humbly request your permission to speak, my queen," she says, and I know from the formal words and respectful tone that things have again changed between us. I wonder if she disapproves of my new life with Caesar.

I take her hands and raise her to her feet. "Charmion, I'm so glad you've come. I've longed to talk to you. So much has happened!"

"You had only to send for me, mistress," she says with a note of reproach.

"You're right," I concede with a sigh. "But everything is so much different with Caesar in my life. Nothing is quite what I expected. Though my brother is now officially my husband, I dislike him more than ever, and he is even less fond of me."

"I know. And that is why I have come today, my queen. To beg you to excuse me from performing tonight at your banquet."

"But I need to have at least one friend there!" I cry.

"You have Caesar!" For a moment we gaze at each other. Then she says, "As you wish, my queen. I shall dance."

The banquet is scarcely bearable. I regret asking Charmion to do something she does not want to do. My brother-husband gets drunk and vomits. I can hardly wait for it to end so that I can shut myself in my quarters. I do not even want to talk to Caesar.

But later that night when Caesar comes to my rooms, I open the door to him and welcome him into my embrace.

Chapter 49

Arsinoë

I wish I could say that matters turn out well, but they do not. My marriage to Ptolemy XIII is little more than a month old, but we can scarcely tolerate the sight of each other.

He is the least of my worries. Caesar has learned that the abominable Pothinus smuggled a secret message to Achillas, advising him to march westward to Alexandria from Pelusium with Ptolemy's army. Now Achillas, with twenty thousand Egyptian foot soldiers and a cavalry of two thousand horsemen under his command, approaches the city walls; Caesar's forces number only four thousand Roman soldiers. I had warned him that this was likely to happen, but Caesar is not used to taking advice from a woman—even one who is well acquainted with the warlike nature of men.

Caesar orders Pothinus seized and brought to him. The guards drag him in and fling him at Caesar's feet. Seated at a table studying a scroll, Caesar barely glances at Pothinus, a quivering mass of flesh begging for his life. "You do not deserve to live," Caesar says, and signals the guards. "Take him away."

"Shall we hold him prisoner, sir?" asks the guard in charge.

Caesar, frowning, shakes his head, his attention again on the scroll. "No. Kill him. He is a traitor."

Pothinus weeps piteously as the guards haul him away. Soon after, the guard returns and presents Caesar with a bloody knife. "The blood of the traitor, my lord," he says.

I am present for all of this, and I have not a single moment of regret that Pothinus is dead.

The fighting between Egyptians and Romans goes on month after month. During this awful time, we are all living in the king's palace as the guests—or maybe as the prisoners—of the Roman general: my angry brother-husband, my bewildered younger brother Ptolemy XIV, my haughty sister Arsinoë, soon to be twenty—and I. The twenty-second anniversary of my birth passes unnoticed, although I make special offerings to Isis to honor her festival.

I will be relieved when Ptolemy XIV and Arsinoë finally sail for Cyprus, for my sister has grown increasingly argumentative. "This is all your fault!" she screeches at me. "You seduced Caesar and brought all of this down on us!"

"No, it is not my fault," I tell her wearily. "I have not caused this to happen, and I can do nothing to stop it."

Arsinoë does not listen. I hardly expect her to. But why has Caesar not sent her away?

Her mentor, Ganymede, is clearly behind Arsinoë's rebelliousness. I have underestimated this man. He is of average height and displays an ordinary appearance and on most occasions an unremarkable manner, but his intellect is of the highest order. Ganymede is both cunning and vicious. His loyalty is entirely to himself.

Ganymede helps Arsinoë to escape from the palace. For reasons I cannot fathom, she has become popular among the Egyptians, and soon the crowds are swarming through the streets, shouting her name and proclaiming her their queen and pharaoh.

I am cast aside by my people, while Arsinoë sits in her encampment by the city walls and calls herself queen.

"Surely this is not what my father wanted!" I rave, livid with anger but powerless to change a thing.

Chapter 50

Ganymede

Caesar is absent for days at a time, mounting defensive positions against Achillas and his men, who outnumber Caesar's army five to one. I remain in the king's palace, now Caesar's—for my own safety, Caesar says. Am I Caesar's prisoner or his lover? I am not quite sure.

Irisi makes her usual rounds at the marketplace and reports that Caesar has ordered stone barricades built around the palace quarter. For a while I do feel safer. Then, only days later, Monifa rushes in, breathless and alarmed. "Caesar has sent an expedition into the harbor with orders to set fire to the Egyptian ships anchored there! They are burning, mistress!"

I rush up to the roof of the palace, from which I have a clear view of the spectacle in the harbor. But what I see horrifies me. The fire has spread from the harbor to the shore. Prevailing winds from the north have swept blazing timbers from the burning ships into the royal quarter. A sudden burst of sparks leaps skyward, followed by a massive tongue of fire and a billowing plume of black smoke. I cry out, for I know exactly where those flames are coming from. Alexandria's Great Library is burning.

I send Yafeu to find Charmion. My messenger is gone for such a long time that I fear for his safety as well as hers. Much later, Charmion, smeared with soot, races up the stairs to the roof, where, alone and distraught, I have kept watch for hours.

"I'm so glad you received my message!" I exclaim as we embrace.

"Message? I have no message from you, Cleopatra. But I knew you would need me, and so I came."

She brings me the crushing news that a large part of the Library of Alexandria and much of the world's finest collection of literature, art, and science, hundreds of thousands of papyrus scrolls gathered by my Ptolemy ancestors, has been reduced to a pile of glowing ash.

"No doubt it can be rebuilt, mistress," she says, trying to comfort me. "I am sure you can find ways to replace many of the scrolls."

"And I will," I promise her, "as soon as I am in power again." *Whenever that will be.*

Arsinoë blames Achillas for this disaster. At her encampment she orders the general arrested, tried, and beheaded, all in the space of a single afternoon, and installs Ganymede at the head of the Egyptian forces. Ganymede quickly proves to be an exceptional general—almost as gifted as Caesar. He builds catapults and other war machines and launches a fierce attack on the Roman defenses. At the same time he manages to divert seawater into the underground aqueducts that carry fresh water from the Nile to vast cisterns supplying the entire city. This is far worse in military terms than the burning of the library.

Caesar paces restlessly. "Never have I faced such a clever adversary as this Ganymede!" he fumes, pounding his fist into his palm.

An idea strikes me, and I interrupt his pacing and seize his hands. "Listen to me, my love!" I tell him urgently. "Alexandria is built on limestone. I learned that long ago from Demetrius, my old tutor. Limestone holds water. If you dig into it, Demetrius used to say, you will find fresh water."

Caesar stares at me. Then he sweeps me into his arms, lifts me off my feet, and kisses me hard. "Brilliant, Cleopatra! We shall start digging at once!"

He gathers all the men under his command and orders wells to be dug in every part of the city. As I predicted, he finds an abundance of fresh water—just in time, too, for thirst and panic have already begun to undermine his troops. Within days of the water crisis being resolved, military reinforcements arrive from Rome. Caesar is jubilant.

But his jubilation is short-lived. Ganymede is reportedly rebuilding his burned-out Egyptian navy, commandeering ships from up and down the Mediterranean coast, even resorting to stripping the wooden roofs from houses to build more ships. Caesar and I are dining alone, discussing this development, when Irisi bursts in, tearful and breathless: "My queen," she cries, her voice breaking, "the royal boat! It has been destroyed! Captain Mshai was stabbed to death and his body thrown into the lake. Ganymede has ordered his men to use the wood from your boat to build his own warship."

I have scarcely taken in the devastating news when a messenger informs Caesar that Ganymede's navy is preparing to attack. "At sunrise tomorrow, my lord," says the messenger.

"How is this possible?" I want to know. "It is almost beyond belief that he has the ships for such an attack!"

"And the foolhardiness to try it," Caesar replies angrily. He calls for a servant to bring him his cloak of imperial purple. "This is the battle that will end the war," he declares, fastening the gold clasp.

It is all happening too fast. "I pray for your safety, my lord," I whisper.

"You have nothing to fear on my behalf, Cleopatra," he says, and kisses me hurriedly. "Tomorrow at this time, we shall celebrate my victory." He strides from the room, the purple cloak swirling behind him.

What does your victory mean? I wonder, staring after him. *That I shall again be queen?*

I dare not think the unthinkable: *And what if you lose?*

Chapter 51

The Battle

When the door has closed behind Caesar, I scarcely know what to do next. Irisi, seeing her duty, takes my hand and urges, "Come, mistress. It is best to sleep while you can."

But sleep is impossible, given the circumstances. I am on the roof of the palace well before sunrise, ready to observe the battle from this vantage point. It is both terrible and thrilling to watch. The adversaries are well matched, but I am confident that Caesar will triumph. *Is he not the greatest general in the world?*

The fighting goes on all day, the advantage shifting from Caesar's ships to Ganymede's and back again. Catapults hurl rocks, and men raise ramps to board enemy ships for hand-to-hand combat. In the smoke and din and confusion it is impossible to determine who is winning the battle.

Charmion somehow manages to find a way into the palace

and comes to keep watch with me. I am grateful for her company. She tries to coax me to eat something, but I have no appetite. When Caesar does not return by the time servants begin to light the lamps, I fear the worst. Charmion and I sit and stare at each other numbly as water drips monotonously through the clepsydra, the water clock, and still there is no word of Caesar.

More hours pass, and I send out servants to inquire, but no one knows anything. I am wracked with worry. Charmion offers to massage my shoulders, and I allow it.

"I believe that you truly love this man," Charmion says, her fingers gently coaxing the stiffness from my neck.

"I do. I love him with every part of my being!" In my weariness and worry I begin to reveal my feelings. Merely speaking Caesar's name gives me comfort and pleasure. "Years ago, when I was very young, I felt desire for Marcus Antonius, the cavalry commander. Do you remember him?"

"Of course I do! He was so handsome!"

"Yes, he was, but I never thought much about real love until I met Caesar," I tell her. In whispers I confide my most profound desire: "Though he is more than thirty years older than I, I wish to become Caesar's wife."

"But does he not already have a wife?" Charmion asks. "And are you not the wife of Ptolemy XIII?"

With a grimace I brush aside the mention of my brother-husband. "You know that Ptolemy is not really a husband—he is still a boy. That situation can be dealt with, if Caesar chooses to do so. Caesar forced us together, and Caesar can surely force us apart. But you are right—he has a wife in Rome. Her name is Calpurnia. His first wife, Cornelia, bore him his only child, Julia, and both are dead. He divorced his second wife, Pompeia, when he suspected her of adultery. 'The wife of Caesar must be above reproach,' he told me. And now there is Calpurnia. 'A fine woman,' he says, and I have no doubt of that. But she is barren and has given him no children, no son to carry on his name. And that grieves him deeply."

My tongue is loose now. We are no longer young girls confiding childish secrets, but grown women. Our lives are widely separated by our circumstances, but we share a deep bond of affection for each other. I know that I can trust Charmion, and I continue to open my heart to her.

"Perhaps," I suggest, "there's some charm that will cause him to forget Calpurnia and stay here with me."

"I'll ask my mother," she promises. "She's an expert in such matters."

I feel encouraged. Lady Amandaris kept my father's love for twenty years. Now, if the gods are willing—and if he has miraculously survived the battle—she will show me how to keep Caesar's.

Sometime in the darkest hour of the night, when I have nearly given up hope, there is a loud clatter and the sound of voices below. Charmion and I rush down from the rooftop as Caesar stumbles in, exhausted but mostly unharmed, and I fly into his arms. Charmion discreetly disappears. I help my lover out of his clothes—his purple cloak is torn and muddy—and call for sponges and a basin of warm water. While I gently wash his bruised and aching body, he describes what happened.

"I leaped overboard into the harbor, and I was forced to hold my cloak in my teeth, dragging it through the water as I swam, lest it fall into the hands of my enemies. They would have been pleased to display it as a trophy of my defeat, and perhaps of my death." He laughs and continues, "As if that were not enough, I also had to carry valuable papers above my head with one hand while I swam with the other. I wish you could have seen it, Cleopatra! Tonight we celebrate the defeat of Ganymede and the complete destruction of his navy. Victory is ours—let us enjoy it, my love!"

But the celebration must be delayed. Mighty Caesar surrenders to exhaustion. He has fallen asleep.

Chapter 52

Ptolemy XIV

Ganymede's Egyptian navy has been demolished, but our challenges—Caesar's and mine—are not yet over.

Throughout countless days of Caesar's battles, first against Achillas and then Ganymede, Ptolemy XIII has been kept a virtual prisoner in another part of the palace. But now a delegation of Egyptians arrives to meet secretly with Caesar, requesting that my brother-husband be released and allowed to reign in place of Arsinoë.

"The people are tired of this woman, who declared herself queen, and of Ganymede, who has raised our taxes yet again to finance his battles," complains the spokesman for the delegation. "Give us Ptolemy XIII as our king and the strife will end."

I would reject their proposal at once and offer them the only sensible solution: I, Cleopatra VII, am their legitimate queen.

But Caesar promises to consider their request, and that

angers me. "It would be to your advantage," Caesar tells me after they have gone and before I can rebuke him. "If I release Ptolemy and he assumes the throne, then you will be restored as queen."

I do not think my brother can be trusted, and I doubt that it is worth the risk. "He has turned fourteen. He's still only a boy, though he thinks he's a man." I try to keep my voice calm and reasonable, though I am raging inside.

Caesar dismisses my objection and calls for Ptolemy to be brought to him. Caesar orders me to wait out of sight, concealed behind a heavy drapery, and to observe their conversation. Can he not see how this infuriates me? Nevertheless, I obey.

Ptolemy falls to his knees, weeping before Caesar and begs to be allowed to stay at the palace. "I have become greatly attached to you, my lord," he declares fervently, clutching at Caesar's robe.

I believe this is all an act, but I must remain silent and hidden.

Caesar insists that Ptolemy must leave and stay in his own quarters, telling him, "We shall part as friends, and we shall soon be reunited as friends." I watch as the two embrace—one I love and one I detest—an uneasy feeling churning in my stomach.

I was right not to trust him. Ptolemy is like a lion released from confinement. He loses no time taking up the war against his mentor and "friend" Caesar, rushing off to the fortified city of Pelusium and assuming the leadership of the Egyptian army. As soon as Caesar learns about this, he is off in furious pursuit of Ptolemy, calling upon his allies for help. The fighting resumes.

I could have told him this would happen, but Caesar does not listen to me.

And then it is over, as suddenly as it began. Trying to flee from the attackers, Ptolemy boards a boat to cross a branch of the Nile. The overloaded ship sinks and Ptolemy is drowned. This brings an end to the war. Should I feel sorrow for the death of my brother-husband? I do not. He would not have hesitated to order my death, if he had the chance.

Caesar returns to Alexandria in triumph, carrying the heavy gold armor retrieved from the muddy waters of the Nile that proves Ptolemy's death. Caesar's next order is for his officers to sweep into Arsinoë's camp and take the "pharaoh" and her general, Ganymede, prisoner. Once again, Caesar and I prepare to celebrate victory. My two enemies—brother and sister—now eliminated, I should feel triumphant, but I am still uneasy.

Perfumed and dressed in my most beguiling gown, I welcome Caesar as my lover and my hero. He gathers me in his arms, remarking, "Now you shall reign as queen, my darling. But as queen you must have a king."

For one exultant moment I believe that Caesar himself wants to be king and that he is suggesting our marriage—all exactly as I had wished! Calpurnia is far, far away in Rome, and Caesar is here at my side. We will marry, we will rule Egypt together, and I will give him the sons he never had. Someday he may even learn to heed my advice.

But in the few months we have been together, I have learned to read Caesar's moods very well, and I see at once—or perhaps I feel it or hear it in his tone—that our marriage is not at all what he intends. I thank the gods that I have kept silent and not revealed my deep desires.

I draw back from his embrace. "Ptolemy XIII is dead. What would you have me do?"

"Marry the brother who lives," he says. "It is nothing more than a pretense, but a necessary one."

I move away from him, stating firmly, "I do not wish to do this, Caesar."

He looks at me in a way that tells me he is quite aware of my feelings and they mean very little to him. "Many of us in power must do things we'd rather not, Cleopatra," he says, mildly enough, but I know that, at least for now, I must do as Caesar says.

Once again, I go through the motions of marrying. Ptolemy XIV and I place our signatures as required to rule Egypt as "the Father-Loving, Brother/Sister Loving Gods," a title I have chosen. My new husband is barely thirteen; I am twenty-two. But Ptolemy XIV is of a different temperament from his older brother, and I believe he will not cause difficulties. In any case, I make certain that my name appears first on the official documents, as it always will. There is another marriage celebration that pleases the people but means nothing at all to me.

Part X

Queen Cleopatra

Egypt in my twenty-second year

Chapter 53

The Queen's Boat

It is the third month of Harvest, the fourth month of my twenty-second year, and I am the acknowledged queen of Egypt. Caesar has promised to provide the backing of three Roman legions to preserve the peace. My new brother-husband, the youngest Ptolemy, meekly does as he is told.

But the battles have taken their toll on Caesar. He grows feverish and raving and requires much tender care, which I am happy to provide. He forbids me to send for a physician, not wishing to let him know that mighty Caesar suffers any weakness. Irisi and Monifa are both knowledgeable in the uses of herbs and charms, and among us we bring him back to full health.

Every morning, Caesar's barber comes to shave him and to dress his hair. He is sensitive about his thinning hair. "It makes me look old," he complains, and I try to persuade him that it does not. This is a small lie. In fact, Caesar looks every one of his fifty-three years.

My future with Caesar remains bright, and my love for him grows deeper as the days and nights go by. Then, one day, he begins to talk about returning to Rome. "My responsibilities are there, dear Cleopatra," he says. "I hold the highest office. I must go back, and soon."

"Of course you must, my love." Though his words have profoundly shocked me, I take Caesar's hand and raise it to my lips. I make up my mind to delay Caesar's departure for Rome by whatever means I can, for as long as I can. Perhaps he will ask me to join him there. We will divide our time between our two countries. We will find a way to be together.

One evening when the two of us have been dining quietly, as we both prefer, Caesar remarks, "For some time I have been curious about the source of the Nile. I've heard that its great length makes it the longest river known, with its headwaters buried deep in the heart of this dark continent. What can you tell me of its origins?"

"No one knows for certain." I pause and pop a sweet into his mouth. "It might be possible to follow it a part of the way. If not to its very source, as you desire, then at least as far as the First Cataract. It would please me to show you the splendors of my country."

Caesar leans closer. "With you, dearest Cleopatra, it will be delightful beyond imagining."

Now I believe I have the way to keep Caesar by my side.

The problem is that Ganymede seized the royal boat and dismembered it to build his warship. A new royal boat, the queen's boat, must be constructed—and quickly.

I could simply assign the task of hiring naval architects and builders to my grand vizier, but I decide to undertake the task myself. I summon Demetrius. My old tutor walks now with the aid of a cane, his body bent under the accumulation of years, but his eyes still gleam with intelligence, and his spirit remains as strong as ever.

He bows with stiffened joints. "How may I serve you, my queen?"

"I want a new royal boat constructed, the most exquisitely luxurious craft ever to travel the waters of the Nile. I will spare no expense for such a boat, but it must be done with all haste. I feel sure, my good Demetrius, that you are well acquainted with experts at the Museion who can design this boat and know of people who will build it for me."

Demetrius smiles. He is missing several teeth. "I shall be glad to assist you, my queen. If you will accompany me to the Museion, we can interrupt the philosophers and find a man of practical knowledge."

I have not visited the Museion in many months, and I enjoy going there with Demetrius. We find a group of architects discussing the damage to the great Library of Alexandria and how to rebuild it. From among them, Demetrius points out two or three experienced in the art of boat building. The men gather around me as I describe my vision of the queen's boat, down to the color of the sails and the design of the jeweled plates and golden goblets.

"And it must all be accomplished in secret. Caesar must not hear of this!"

The architects say, "Yes, yes, of course, my queen. Everything shall be as you wish."

"What do you think?" I ask Demetrius afterward. "Are they as good as their word?"

"They are," says the tutor. "But I cannot help asking, why this hurry? Your father spent a year building his royal boat, and you want it done in a fraction of that time."

"Caesar speaks of returning to Rome," I tell him. "I want him to see Egypt before he leaves, to feel about my country as strongly as I do."

Demetrius looks at me thoughtfully, his head tilted to one side. "You do it, then, for love."

"For love of Egypt," I tell him, though he is right, and he knows it.

Chapter 54

Farewell Journey

Ignoring the grumbling that the queen's boat has taken precedence over reconstruction of the Library of Alexandria and rebuilding of a city severely damaged by fighting, I meet almost daily with architects, engineers, and builders.

As work progresses, I begin to search for a captain. As I had known to my great sorrow, the elder Captain Mshai was murdered by Ganymede. But his son who sailed with me to Ashkelon would be a fine choice. "It is my honor to serve you, Queen Cleopatra," the younger Mshai says, and we immediately reach an agreement.

The race to finish the boat accelerates as Caesar's restlessness grows. When Caesar again speaks of his duties to the Roman senate, muttering, "I have tarried here longer than perhaps I should," I send an urgent message to the boat builders, instructing them that in ten days' time I will come to inspect my new boat. Accomplishing it all in secret, they remind me, has greatly complicated the project.

"There will be a large reward to each of you if the boat is completely finished by the time of my arrival." I do not mention the consequences of *not* finishing in time, but these men certainly remember my father and his often cruel methods of inspiring his subjects to do exactly what he wanted.

For ten days I steer my conversations with Caesar away from any mention of responsibilities, duties, home. Then I summon Charmion.

"I know why you have sent for me, my queen," she says, even before I say anything. "I did as you asked me and spoke to my mother about your wish for some sort of charm to keep Caesar from returning to Rome."

"What did Lady Amandaris say, Charmion?" I ask eagerly. "Does she have a special charm, an amulet, a spell that will help me?"

Charmion shakes her head. "I am truly sorry to disappoint you, mistress. My mother tells me there is nothing you can do, no clever scheme you can devise, that will keep Caesar from leaving you. He will go back to Rome, if that is what he believes he must do. But his heart will remain with you. You have cast your spell on him, Cleopatra, as you will cast your spell on every man you desire! For as long as Caesar lives, he will always love you, even though he is far away." She kneels before me, and our faces are so close together, they are almost touching. "Just as King Ptolemy loved my mother, even through the long years when he was far from her, far from Alexandria."

I allow myself a deep sigh. "Thank you, Charmion. This is

not what I wish to hear, but please thank Lady Amandaris for her wisdom."

I wipe away a few tears, and then I compose myself and clap my hands, signaling to my servants for refreshments.

On the day I have fixed for my visit to the new boat, I tell Caesar, "Dearest love, I have a surprise for you."

Caesar, I have learned, is not fond of surprises—he prefers to believe that he is always in control—but, nevertheless, he is curious to see what I have prepared for him. I call for our chairs and our bearers, and we are carried swiftly to Lake Mareotis. Though I have been monitoring progress carefully at each step, this will be my first visit to the finished project, with every sail, every cushion, every goblet in place. I am anxious—what if it does not live up to my expectations? What if Caesar shrugs off my greatest effort to please him?

But the moment we arrive on the shore of the lake and glimpse the splendor of the gilded boat reflecting the rays of the Sun God Ra, I know that I have achieved a great success. The queen's boat is magnificent, even more splendid than its predecessor. "I ordered this to be built in your honor," I tell him.

"It is beyond anything I could imagine," he exclaims, taking my hand, and he shows his delight repeatedly as we wander from deck to deck, admiring each exquisite detail. "When do we sail, my darling?"

"Whenever it pleases you, my lord."

Caesar takes me in his arms, tells me how beautiful I am, and kisses me passionately. I sense his determination to leave for Rome is weakening—but only for an hour, a day, a month at most. I know, even at this moment, that no matter how much Caesar loves me or what I do, I cannot keep him with me for long—not now, and maybe not ever.

Days later, we leave Alexandria together and begin our journey up the Nile. At every stop we greet the governors and priests and make offerings to the gods. Caesar is happy to become acquainted with the land and the people who have come under his protection and my rule. And he relishes the sights as I point them out to him: the Great Pyramids, the Sphinx, the temple to Hathor built in Dendara by my father, just as he promised. We view the colossal statues and gigantic pylons at Thebes, even the half-buried temple of Hatshepsut.

Finally, we reach the sacred island of Philae, watched over by Isis, the goddess I revere most deeply. A part of the god Osiris, her husband, was buried here before Isis gathered up the pieces and made him whole again. I show Caesar the pylon built by my father, proudly pointing out the scenes of Ptolemy XII killing his enemies under the eternal gaze of Isis and her son, Horus.

Beyond Philae lies the First Cataract, and we must turn back. Although I recognize that once we reach Alexandria, Caesar will leave for Rome, I give Mshai the order to return. But before the queen's boat leaves Philae, I make a special offering to Isis, praying that I will one day bear Caesar a son.

Almost as soon as we arrive in Alexandria I am surprised to discover—though I should not be—that even before we left on our idyllic journey, Caesar had ordered the preparation and provisioning of a ship to carry him back to Rome. The ship is ready and waiting, and Caesar is determined. And so, only days after the end of our journey together, we are saying good-bye.

I promised myself that I would not weep when Caesar left, but I break that promise almost at once. My tears must always be shed in private—the price of being a queen, a pharaoh, semidivine, above human weakness. Through the farewell banquets and ceremonies, I remain stoic and regal, the queen of my people, as I want my lover to remember me.

When the hour comes for his departure, Caesar and I hold each other in one last, silent embrace. We have no words left to say that have not been said before. He steps into the small gilded boat I have given him and is rowed out to his waiting ship, its yellow sails as brilliant as the Egyptian sun.

Seated on a throne by the water's edge, I watch the ship leave the Great Harbor. The crowd disperses, but I cannot bear to return to the palace just yet. I order my bearers to carry my royal chair over the causeway to the lighthouse. From there I gaze out at the dark sea until the last bright dot of yellow vanishes beyond the horizon.

Epilogue

Alexandria, in my thirty-ninth year

Seventeen years have passed since Caesar sailed for Rome. I knew on that day that I would soon bear his child. Today, as I look back on our two months on Egypt's great Nile River, I remember a time of love and discovery, a time of triumph. Now the triumph is long past, the love brought to a tragic end by the murder of Caesar as he met with the Roman senate three years later. I cannot forget the horror of that day—the fifteenth of March in 44 B.C. on your calendar—as Caesar's enemies set upon him and stabbed him twenty-three times. His closest friend and general, Marcus Antonius, detained outside the senate chamber, was powerless to stop it.

At the time of Caesar's assassination I was in Rome with our three-year-old son, Ptolemy XV Caesar, born soon after Caesar left Egypt. Antonius grieved with me at our mutual loss and did what he could to help me, swearing vengeance upon Caesar's assassins. Within the month, my son and I left Rome and returned to Egypt. Roman law did not allow Caesar to acknowledge the boy, called Caesarion—Little Caesar—as his own. Instead, he named his great-nephew, Octavian, as his heir. I was not even mentioned in his will. In the beginning I harbored no ill will toward Octavian. But events have made him my enemy, and it is Octavian who now waits at my doorstep, demanding to be brought to me. It is Octavian who would take me to Rome in chains, to humiliate me.

On the day I left Rome fourteen years ago, Marcus Antonius came to bid me farewell. "We will meet again, Queen Cleopatra," he said, bowing low in the Egyptian manner. "I promise you on my honor."

I came home to Alexandria to mourn. My fifteen-year-old brother-husband, Ptolemy XIV, had been left in charge during my absence, but within months he was dead. I was blamed for his death, though I deny all responsibility. Caesarion was declared king of Egypt, and I ruled as his regent. I now had absolute power, and for the next several years I worked hard to bring prosperity to my country, despite continuing crop failures. But I needed protection, and this is when Marcus Antonius fulfilled his promise and entered my life once again. At his command I sailed to Tarsus to meet him. Inevitably, we became lovers. Our life together is another story, but there is no time left for me to tell it. I leave it to others to tell for me.

Octavian's friend and then his bitter rival, Antonius has shared my crushing defeat. Just days ago, he died in my arms.

"Cleopatra," he said as the life left him, "you are as beautiful now as you were when I first met you. You have always been the queen of my heart."

I bathed his dear face with my tears. "In life nothing could part us from each other, dearest love, but in death we will be parted forever." I am not certain he heard my last whispered words.

Now Octavian refuses to wait any longer. He demands that I surrender my treasure and myself. Nothing less will satisfy him.

I have anticipated this moment and made my decision. I will not allow myself to be taken prisoner. Irisi prepared a bath of scented waters and helped me dress in my most elegant gown, my most precious jewels, and the royal diadem. I have dined on a splendid meal. Charmion, my faithful friend for so many years, has brought me the basket of figs as I requested.

"Charmion," I tell her, "the time has come."

I embrace Irisi and Charmion and lie down on my golden couch. Charmion, weeping, removes the lid of the basket. Venomous cobras writhe among the figs. I reach for the largest snake and hold it to my breast. Twin droplets of blood appear where its fangs have pierced my flesh and released their deadly venom.

Cleopatra in History

Cleopatra may be the most famous queen in history, and yet beyond a few basic facts of her life, her love affairs, and her children, almost nothing is documented. The exact date of her birth is unknown. The identity of her mother is unknown. There are no eyewitness accounts of her life, and no contemporary records survive to tell her story—fire and flood have destroyed them all. Most of what we do know about Cleopatra has been pieced together from the writings of two ancient historians: Plutarch, author of *Life of Antony*, who was born seventy-six years after Cleopatra's death, and Cassius Dio, whose *Roman History*, written in the third century, supplies additional information, some of it reliable, some not.

In modern times archaeologists, historians, biographers, novelists, and filmmakers all depend to some degree on theory and supposition, filling in the blank spaces with a great deal of imagination. One of the most intriguing mysteries is the identity of Cleopatra's mother. She may have been a Ptolemy, closely related to Cleopatra's Greek ancestors, or she may have been of elite Egyptian background with a genetic makeup having its source in many different parts of the Mediterranean world. Some anthropologists claim that Cleopatra's mother was a dark-skinned Nubian; most agree that Cleopatra's skin tone was probably olive or light brown.

The return of Cleopatra and Julius Caesar to Alexandria after their cruise on the Nile ends an early chapter of Cleopatra's life, in Year 5 of her rule, 47 B.C. in our calendar. As she anticipated, Caesar left for Rome almost immediately, taking with him Arsinoë and Ganymede as prisoners.

A short time later, Cleopatra gave birth to a boy she named Ptolemy XV Caesar, whom the people of Egypt called Caesarion, assuming that he was Caesar's son. Cleopatra was not only a reigning pharaoh and therefore semidivine in the eyes of the Egyptian people; she was now also a mother—in her own eyes the earthly incarnation of Isis, the goddess of motherhood.

For the next year Cleopatra ruled Egypt with her brother-husband Ptolemy XIV, while Caesar pursued wars in Hispania (present-day Spain), Africa, and Asia Minor against the followers of his late friend-turned-enemy, Pompey. In 46 B.C., Caesar returned victorious from battle and sent for Cleopatra to join him. She made the long voyage with Caesarion and Ptolemy XIV. Caesar welcomed all three and installed them at his country estate outside Rome.

How long Cleopatra stayed as Caesar's guest is not clear. He did, after all, have a wife, Calpurnia, who surely was not pleased by her husband's visitor. The Romans, too, disapproved of this exotic foreigner, believing the Egyptian queen was leading Caesar into decadent ways. When Caesar left again, Cleopatra may have decided that she needed to make her presence felt in Egypt. She made a trip to Alexandria with Ptolemy XIV and returned to Rome without him when Caesar came home from his wars in the summer of 45 B.C.

During her time in Rome, Cleopatra renewed her acquaintance with the handsome cavalry commander who had caught her eye some years earlier: Marcus Antonius, now Caesar's right-hand man, known more familiarly now to English speakers as Mark Antony.

Caesar may have tired of leading troops into battle, but he had not tired of the idea of being the great leader. He aspired to be king, to sit on a golden throne, to wear a royal diadem. Mark Antony supported him in this desire, but many others opposed him. In 44 B.C., on the Ides of March—March 15 was the day on which debts were traditionally settled in Rome—Caesar's enemies attacked him on the floor of the theater where the Roman senate was to meet and stabbed him to death.

Caesar's assassination was a terrible blow to Cleopatra, who had to deal not only with the loss of her lover but with the knowledge that their son, Caesarion, was not named as Caesar's heir and Cleopatra herself was not even mentioned in his will. Instead, his great-nephew, Gaius Octavius, later known as Octavian, was adopted as his son and named his heir and successor. Within a month of Caesar's death, Cleopatra left Rome with Caesarion, bound for Alexandria. There she found that fifteen-year-old Ptolemy XIV had taken over as pharaoh. Months later, Ptolemy XIV was dead—poisoned, some say, by Cleopatra—and three-year-old Caesarion became King Ptolemy XV, with his mother ruling Egypt as his regent and queen.

Despite continuing low floods and poor harvests, life in Egypt became relatively peaceful. Meanwhile, back in Rome, Octavian and Mark Antony were in power, and they asked for Cleopatra's help in punishing the assassins responsible for Caesar's murder. Cleopatra responded by sending back the Roman legions Caesar had left in Egypt. In return the Romans recognized Caesarion as the rightful king of Egypt and Cleopatra as queen.

Without Caesar, Cleopatra and Caesarion were vulnerable and needed protection. Egypt was suffering a dire shortage of grain, and famine stalked the land, but with a wealth of natural resources at her disposal—gems, gold, and minerals—Cleopatra was still the richest queen in the world. Mark Antony needed the wealth that Egypt could provide.

The former cavalry commander summoned Queen Cleopatra to meet him in the city of Tarsus in Asia Minor. With her usual dramatic flair, she arrived in a gilded ship with silver oars and purple sails, as splendid as the boat on which she and Caesar had once floated down the Nile. Declining Antony's invitation to dine with him, she invited him aboard her ship as her honored guest. At the end of the lavish banquet she presented Antony with the golden plates on which the meal had been served. Like Caesar at his first meeting with Cleopatra, Antony was entranced by her considerable charms. The two became lovers.

When Cleopatra returned to Egypt in the winter of 41/40 B.C., Antony soon followed. Perhaps they made a celebration of Cleopatra's twenty-ninth birthday, and at around the same time, his forty-second. The pair were inseparable, and less than a year later, Cleopatra gave birth to twins, named Alexander and Cleopatra. But by then Antony was gone.

Mark Antony already had a wife, Fulvia. (He had been married several times.) Even after Fulvia died, he seemed in no hurry to return to Alexandria and the arms of Cleopatra. We can only speculate on how Cleopatra must have felt when, in order to show his loyalty to Octavian, Antony married Octavian's half-sister, Octavia.

After a separation of some three years, during which Cleopatra succeeded in putting her country on sound financial footing,

Antony again sent for her. His relationship with Octavian had soured, and he needed the queen's help. Their meeting took place in Antioch, in the winter of 37/36 B.C. Antony acknowledged the twins as his own, the old flame was reignited, and Antony and Cleopatra became lovers once more. Nine months later Cleopatra bore another son, named Ptolemy Philadelphus. By then she had bargained control away from Antony of major portions of the eastern Mediterranean, and she returned to Alexandria in triumph.

Not surprisingly, Antony's marriage of convenience to Octavia, mother of two of his children, was coming apart. Antony chose to stay in Alexandria with Cleopatra, where the two occupied gold and silver thrones with their various children ranged around them. Not everyone was favorably impressed by this display. Among those whose opposition was most outspoken was Octavian.

For several years the two lovers, Antony and Cleopatra, enjoyed the good life in Alexandria while the two rivals, Antony and Octavian, engaged in a war of words. It was inevitable that the rivals would meet in actual battle. Cleopatra pledged to assist Antony, and they began to build a fleet. By late 32 B.C. Antony and Cleopatra had assembled an army of infantry and cavalry and a navy of five hundred warships—Cleopatra herself commanded a fleet of sixty ships—and they waited for Octavian to make his move. It came late in the summer of 31 B.C. at the battle of Actium, which ended with Antony's humiliating defeat.

Cleopatra hurried back to Alexandria and made an entrance into the city as though she were victorious. Unable to gather support for his cause from his discouraged troops, Antony brooded in solitude for a while before returning to Cleopatra's palace. Both realized the end was near. Cleopatra hoped to abdicate in favor of her son, Caesarion—by 30 B.C. he was sixteen, of age to rule—and of Antony's son, Antyllus. Octavian notified Cleopatra that he might agree to this only if she had Antony killed. When lavish gifts and bribery failed to sway Octavian, Antony challenged Octavian to one more battle. But at the crucial moment Antony's men deserted him, and the once famous warrior was soundly defeated.

Retreating once more to Alexandria, where Cleopatra had taken refuge in her treasure-filled tomb, Antony was told that Cleopatra had committed suicide. At this news Antony stabbed himself, only to learn as he lay bleeding that his beloved was not dead after all. Too weak to move, he had his servants carry him to the tomb and haul him up by ropes to a high window. Antony died in Cleopatra's arms.

Octavian permitted Cleopatra to arrange Antony's funeral. Then, rather than allow Octavian to take her prisoner and return with her to Rome as his trophy, she chose to end her own life.

Like most other facts of the queen's history, Cleopatra's manner of death is still debated. Only the date is certain: August 12, 30 B.C. According to Plutarch, writing more than a century later, Octavian "gave orders that her body should be buried with Anthony's in splendid and regal fashion."

This left Cleopatra's sixteen-year-old son Caesarion to rule as Ptolemy XV, but he was captured and executed, and on August 31 Octavian annexed Egypt as a Roman province. Taking the name Caesar Augustus, Octavian had himself declared the first emperor of the Roman Empire. Cleopatra's three children by Mark Antony were taken to Rome as prisoners and eventually given to Antony's wife Octavia to raise.

Thus ended the life of Egypt's greatest queen and began the enduring legend of Cleopatra.

A Note from the Author

Was Cleopatra beautiful?

People who know of my interest in the Egyptian queen often ask me that. There are no portraits of her. Paintings on temple walls thought to be of Cleopatra are highly stylized. Most sculptures are damaged or cannot be positively identified. Her images on coins are worn to a blur. So, was she a classic beauty, or did she have the long hooked nose, bony chin, and thin lips of a witch, as some say? What about those Venus rings, rolls of fat sometimes visible around her neck, indicating pudginess? Was she a woman of color, with an African mother or grandmother, as some people claim, or was she purely Greek? Have we any idea what she really looked like?

The truth is that nobody actually knows, although recently, computer imagery has provided some ideas. For many years my own mental picture of Cleopatra coincided with shots of Elizabeth Taylor playing the role of the ancient queen in a 1963 movie. I know now that mental picture was wide of the mark. But no matter what her physical appearance, Cleopatra was certainly a charming and brilliant woman who fascinated two Roman conquerors and continues to fascinate modern students and readers.

Not long ago, I traveled to Egypt in search of the last queen. I floated down the same Nile that Cleopatra traveled with Julius

Caesar, and I visited some of the same sites—the Great Pyramids, the temples of Thebes—that were ancient even in her day, more than two thousand years ago. And I explored the modern city of Alexandria. There is not much to see of the ancient one. In 2002 the new Bibliotheca Alexandrina replaced the original great Library of Alexandria that was partially destroyed by fire in Cleopatra's time. In the centuries following Cleopatra's death, the Library was attacked and finally destroyed. The dramatic new one was built near the site of the original.

The Pharos lighthouse that guided ships into the Great Harbor is long gone, badly damaged and eventually obliterated by earthquakes. But four centuries after Cleopatra's death it was the undersea earthquake and the tsunami, as we now call it, which followed that submerged most of ancient Alexandria. The royal quarter, the palaces, and all the artifacts that could be associated with the last queen's life now lie many feet below the surface in the murky waters of the Great Harbor.

Underwater archaeologists have explored these waters, bringing up more than six thousand items—granite heads, silver coins, pottery, and other artifacts—and these scientists believe that many thousands more are scattered over the harbor floor. At the end of 2009, divers hauled to the surface a pylon more than seven feet tall and weighing nine tons. They believe it is part of the temple of Isis, the goddess with whom Cleopatra identified so strongly.

The Egyptian government now plans to build an underwater museum with tunnels that will allow visitors to view these sunken treasures of history. Even more recently, archaeologists believe they have found the long-lost tomb where Antony and Cleopatra lie buried, some thirty miles west of Alexandria.

I hope to return to Egypt someday to get a closer look at Cleopatra's world. But my guess is that even after the archaeologists have finished their digging, the historians have completed their studies, and the anthropologists have run their computer analyses, Queen Cleopatra VII of Egypt will remain as much a mystery as ever.

Carolyn Meyer

About the Research for This Book:

Researching is always much easier than writing—and that's a fact! Until the day the final draft is finished, there is always the temptation to search for one more source, one more book to read, another detail to track down on the Internet, or another fact to check, and to delay the challenging task of structuring the story, developing the characters, imagining the scenes, and finding the voice, all the while maintaining historical accuracy.

My methods are highly personal. I start by searching the online catalogs of the university and public libraries in my city. I check out the books that seem most useful, take quick notes, and decide if I want to own them. Then I order the ones I want and make a mess of them with underlining, highlighting, and sticky notes. The books listed in the bibliography have been subjected to this treatment, and they stayed on my desk as I wrote. Stacy Schiff's masterful *Cleopatra: A Life* had not yet been published, or it would certainly have been among my first purchases. But I find that historians and biographers often disagree on even the most basic facts (the identity of Cleopatra's mother is one example), and I must pick and choose how best to tell the story without rewriting history.

Many questions come up in the process, and so at every step I begin an Internet search: names for minor (invented) characters, an explanation of the Egyptian calendar, a description of the Nilometer, for instance. Not all sites seem well documented or reliable. Most I click, take what I need, delete, and move on. Those that proved useful I bookmarked for future reference and are listed here.

All of this is happening during the months that I am thinking, visualizing, imagining, writing, checking the facts, rewriting, tossing out, starting over, and refining—until it's finished.

Bibliography

Chauveau, Michel. *Egypt in the Age of Cleopatra*. Translated by David Lorton. Ithaca and London: Cornell University Press, 2000.

Foreman, Laura. *Cleopatra's Palace: In Search of a Legend*. New York: Discovery Books, 1999.

Mertz, Barbara. *Red Land, Black Land: Daily Life in Ancient Egypt*. New York: William Morris, 2008.

Nelles Map of Egypt. Munich: Nelles Verlag GmbH, 2007.

Roller, Duane W. *Cleopatra: A Biography*. New York: Oxford University Press, 2010.

Tyldesley, Joyce. *Cleopatra: Last Queen of Egypt*. London: Profile Books, 2008.

Internet Resources

Ashmawy, Alaa K. "Alexandria." Authentic Wonders. Last modified May 23, 2006. http://www.authenticwonders.com/Alexandria/.

Dollinger, André. "Ancient Egypt: Music and Dance." Last modified October 2009. http://www.reshafim.org.il/ad/egypt/timelines/topics/music.htm.

El-Aref, Nevine. “How Pharaoh Sailed to Karnak.” The Corner Report. Last modified January 12, 2008. http://www.thecornerreport.com/index.php?title=how_pharaoh_sailed_to_karnak&more=1&c=1&tb=1&pb=1.

Grieshaber, Frank. “The Calendar of Ancient Egypt.” Egyptology Online Resources. Accessed July 2008. http://aegyptologie.online-resourcen.de/Calendar_of_Ancient_Egypt.

Hayes, Holly. “Serapeum, Alexandria.” Sacred Destinations. Last modified July 8, 2009. http://www.sacred-destinations.com/egypt/alexandria-serapeum.

Moore, Walter. “Authentic Ancient Egyptian Names.” Accessed March 2009. http://kememou.com/names.html.

Postel, Sandra. *Pillar of Sand: Can the Irrigation Miracle Last?* W.W. New York: Norton Company, 1999. Excerpted online at http://www.waterhistory.org/histories/nile/.

Thompson, James C. “Women in the Ancient World.” Last modified July 2010. http://www.womenintheancientworld.com.

Tour Egypt. “Tour Egypt.” Accessed June 2009. http://www.touregypt.net.

Time Line

117 B.C. Birth of Ptolemy XII
80 B.C. Ptolemy XII becomes king of Egypt
75 B.C. Birth of Tryphaena
73 B.C. Birth of Berenike
69 B.C. Birth of Cleopatra VII
67 B.C. Birth of Arsinoë
61 B.C. Birth of Ptolemy XIII
60 B.C. Birth of Ptolemy XIV; King Ptolemy XII goes to Rome
59 B.C. King returns to Alexandria
58 B.C. Royal family on Nile; King forced into exile; Tryphaena, Berenike usurp throne
57 B.C. Tryphaena disappears; Berenike rules
55 B.C. King returns from exile, orders Berenike's death; Cleopatra becomes queen consort
51 B.C. King Ptolemy XII dies; Cleopatra VII and Ptolemy XIII crowned
48 B.C. Cleopatra flees unrest to Ashkelon; returns to Alexandria
48 B.C. Cleopatra meets Caesar; marries brother Ptolemy XIII; brother dies; marries XIV
47 B.C. Cleopatra, Caesar on Nile journey; Caesar leaves Alexandria; Caesarion born
44 B.C. Cleopatra, Caesarion visit Rome; Caesar assassinated; Octavian named heir

41 B.C. Cleopatra, Marcus Antonius become lovers

40–30 B.C. Cleopatra rules Egypt, prosperity increases; bears Antonius three children

32 B.C. Cleopatra, Antonius assemble fleet; Octavian declares war on Cleopatra

31 B.C. Octavian defeats fleet at battle of Actium

30 B.C. Cleopatra, Antonius die

Egyptian Gods and Goddesses

The ancient Egyptians believed in many gods. Their names changed through time; they often appeared in various forms; they performed various functions. Here are a few of the important ones mentioned in this book, but keep in mind that there were dozens more.

Ra—sometimes spelled Re; also called Amun or Amon; sun god; creator god; greatest of the gods

Dionysus—Greek god of wine; inspirer of ecstasy; favorite of King Ptolemy XII

Serapis—protector of the city of Alexandria; originally Greek; known for healing powers

Osiris—god of the dead; judge of spirits; brother-husband of the goddess Isis

Isis—symbol of devoted wife and mother; goddess of fertility; wife of Osiris; mother of Horus and Hathor

Horus—son of Isis and Osiris; falcon-headed; patron of Egypt

Hathor—daughter of Isis and Osiris; goddess of love and pleasure

Seth—brother of Isis and Osiris; murderer of Osiris

Maat—daughter of Ra; goddess of truth

Neith—goddess of hunting and war; mother of crocodile god, Sobek

Anubis—jackal-headed god; accompanied dead on their journey to the afterlife

Mut—wife of Amun; mother-god

Thoth—god of writing and wisdom; inventor of numbers; often took form of a baboon

Egyptian Calendar

The Egyptian calendar in Ptolemaic times was divided into three seasons of four 30-day months each, with five extra days designated as the Opening of the Year, coinciding with the rising of Sirius, the Dog-Star, around June 21. The seasons had Egyptian names, but I have used the English names, which are easier to follow. The year looked something like this:

Season of Inundation/Flooding

First month: June 15–July 15
Second month: July 15–August 15
Third month: August 15–September 15
Fourth month: September 15–October 15

Season of Emergence/Planting (winter)

First month: October 15–November 15
Second month: November 15–December 15
Third month: December 15–January 15
Fourth month: January 15–February 15

Season of Harvest (summer)

First month: February 15–March 15
Second month: March 15–April 15
Third month: April 15–May 15
Fourth month: May 15–June 15

About the Author

CAROLYN MEYER is the acclaimed author of more than fifty books for young people. Her many award-winning novels include *Mary, Bloody Mary*, an ABA Pick of the Lists, an NCSS-CBC Notable Children's Trade Book in the Field of Social Studies, and an ALA Best Book for Young Adults; and *Marie, Dancing*, a Book Sense Pick. She lives in Albuquerque, New Mexico.